SPEAKING OF LOVE

ASIA MONIQUE

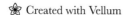

Elena Brooks is the epitome of a good girl with a spark to her that many rarely get to see. She has been taking care of everyone else her entire life, so when she moves to New York and is free to live as she pleases, she has no idea how to spend the time. That is until the captivating Noah White vows to be the one to take care of her for a change.

Noah White is no stranger to love. After the demise of his fourteen-year relationship, he finds himself confused about what's to come. When he meets the bright-eyed, Elena Brooks, he sees everything in her that hadn't been a part of his past.

The two form a friendship that leads them into a direction neither may be ready for but even that doesn't stop them.

Introduction

My first release of the New Year and I have to say that I'm really proud of it. I enjoyed writing Noah + Elena's story. I find it to be beautiful and authentic. Full of honesty and trust. If you've never read a book by me, then you must know that I write for the people who want to get away from everyday life. If you're looking for drama on every page, then this isn't the book for you. With that being said, I hope you enjoy it.

Xoxo, Asia

THE WEDDING...

"By the power invested in me, I now pronounce you husband and wife," the preacher blared. He glanced at Elijah. "You may now kiss your bride." As Elijah leaned in to claim Nova's lips, my eyes found Noah. He was standing behind Elijah's best man, Carter, with his eyes already trained on me. I couldn't resist following the length of his tuxedo-clad body. Noah wasn't the type to get dressed up, but this look on him was becoming my favorite. I slowly moved my gaze upward and settled on his handsome face. His deep umber complexation was glowing under the lights of the hotel's ballroom. I smiled broadly at him, and he winked in reply. I quickly looked away so he couldn't see what the simple gesture had done to me. I wish I could stop the feelings that I'd developed for him, but nothing I did worked.

"Elena, come on, girl," Brynlee murmured, grabbing ahold of my hand. I glanced up at her, but her back was already to me as she pulled me through the two sections of chairs that split the bride's family from the Grooms. Elijah and I didn't have much family, but who needed to be here had shown up and shown out. "Where'd your mind go?"

"Nowhere," I said, smiling at a glowing Brynlee. Marriage had done her good. She squinted at me and shook her head.

"We'll talk another day," she whispered, leaning in to give me a hug as we stood in the hotel lobby. "I know your brother and Nova want to stay out of you and Noah's business, but I'm here. You can always confide in me." I wanted to respond and say thank you. She had no idea how hard it's been keeping my feelings bottled in, but when Noah's voice tickled the back of my neck, I became distracted.

"You guys ready to party?" he asked, kissing the side of my face. Brynlee's eyes connected with mine, and then she lifted her eyes to meet Noah's.

"That's why we splurged on an open bar," she chirped. I chuckled and nodded. That had been the number one priority for us when Nova asked Brynlee and me to help plan her wedding. She'd asked two weeks ago, and we'd been able to make it happen with surprisingly no bumps in the road. Nova was six weeks pregnant and wanted to tie the knot before she started showing and couldn't fit into a decent wedding dress.

"They removed all the chairs," Samir said, approaching. He kissed Brynlee and then focused his attention on Noah and me. "The guests are already inside and waiting."

"I'll go grab my brother and Nova." They nodded and walked off. I kept my eyes on their retreating backs because I didn't want to turn around and face Noah. Having him so close to me was driving me insane.

"Na," he said, placing a hand on my shoulder and

turning me to face him. My heart thumped against my chest. Only he called me, *Na.*

So much for not wanting to face him, I thought.

He peered down at me with a look in his eyes that I couldn't read.

"Are you OK?"

"Yea, I'm OK," I replied, nodding. "Are you?" He nodded and stepped back.

"As long as you are." We stared at each other for what felt like a lifetime. These stare downs happened more often than not.

"I'm going to go—"

"I'll go," he said, cutting me off. "You go meet up with everyone else, and I'll be there in a few with the two love birds." He gave me one last look and then turned away to go find Nova and Elijah. I watched his back until he disappeared around a corner. I took two deep breaths and turned to meet up with the rest of the wedding party with Noah heavy on my mind. I wanted to not like him so bad. I wanted to not be falling in love with him, but it was too late. I was already falling, and I knew that if I didn't get a grip and soon, I'll be falling flat on my face.

THE MUSIC in the ballroom lowered, and all eyes moved toward the front where Carter was standing with a microphone in his hand.

"He's so fine," Isabella, his wife, cooed. I glanced her way and laughed. "I can't believe I married that fine ass man."

"You guys were friends first, right?" I asked as he began to give his best man speech. I'd already had the pleasure of meeting Carter and Isabella before I moved to New York, but I never got to pick her brain about their relationship.

"I've known Elijah since we were eighteen. We were fresh out of high school and over a thousand miles away from home, sharing a dorm...."

"Best friends," she confirmed. "We've known each other since before we could remember." Her eyes stayed on him as she spoke. "He figured out that he was in love with me before I ever did." I nodded and focused on Carter.

"What I've learned about Elijah is that he's fearless, and no matter his circumstances, he'll never fold. Nova, you have a good one. I see nothing but a lifetime of happiness for the two of you." He held his glass up. "Congratulations."

"You know that he won't know how you feel about him until you open your mouth and say something, right?"

"I... what are you talking about?" She stepped in front of me.

"Noah," she said, smiling. "I can tell you like him." I shrugged.

"We're just friends." She chuckled and nodded.

"Sure, you are."

"We are—"

"I do not doubt that you two are friends, but I know there's more." She paused and smiled. "I'm probably overstepping, but I saw the way you two looked at each other on New Year's, and I saw the way you two interacted tonight. There's something there, and if you don't speak up now, then eventually it'll be too late." She turned and walked away, leaving me speechless. I guess she knew from experience, but how could I open up about my feelings when he was still trying to move on from a fourteen-year relationship that ended less than a year ago. I couldn't and wouldn't hurt myself by laying my heart on the line for a man that I knew was emotionally unavailable.

"Elena, come take shots with us," Brynlee yelled from the bar. I shook away my thoughts of a life with Noah and headed her way. As I approached, Juniper tossed an arm over my shoulder and then handed me a shot.

"What is this?" I asked, holding it up.

"Doesn't matter," Magnolia chimed, throwing hers back and picking up another. I looked at the clear liquid again and shrugged before knocking it back. I let the familiar burn of Tequila take over my body and sighed in relief. I would need more of these if that meant it would help take my mind off my stupid feelings.

"Another!"

A few hours later, I was in Noah's arms as he carried me back to my room. I hadn't planned on getting a room, but after drinking a little too much with the flower sisters, there was no way I would make it home in one piece. And when Noah saw me, he made it clear that he wasn't letting me out of his sight tonight.

"I c-could have w-walked," I slurred, tucking my face in the crook of his neck and taking a long whiff of the cologne I loved so much. "You smell really good." The deep rumbled in his chest made me laugh. I opened my eyes to look at him and found nothing but amusement dancing in his eyes.

"You definitely can't walk, Na," he said, focusing his attention in front of us. "And thank you. I try to keep up with my hygiene." I wanted to respond, but the soft cushion of a mattress beneath me pulled my attention to my surroundings.

"When did we get in the room?" He chuckled and shook his head while kneeling in front of me.

"I need to keep you away from the flower sisters," he

murmured, pulling my shoes off my feet. "They've been trouble since we were teens."

"I-I love them," I whispered, lifting my hand to touch his face. He lifted his dark eyes to meet mine and stared. "Have I ever told you how handsome you are?"

"Not that I recall." His eyes were still on mine. I felt as if he were looking straight through me. Like he could see how I felt about him.

"You're really handsome." He smiled.

"And you're beautiful as fuck, Na," he replied. "Now sit still so I can get you situated."

"OK," I whispered, laying back. I stared at the ceiling for what felt like forever. Eventually, Noah was lifting me further onto the bed and placing the blanket over my body. "Will you stay?"

"Never planned on leaving." I watched as he pulled his tie off and removed his shirt. I didn't miss the fact that he'd kept his pants on as he slid into the bed next to me. I also didn't fight him when he pulled my body snug against his.

"Noah."

"Yea?"

"I love you." It wasn't the first time I'd said those words. I didn't have the guts to admit that I loved him as more than just a friend, and I wasn't sure if I'd ever be able to.

"I love you too, Na," he said, yawning. "Get some sleep." As if my body needed to hear him say it, I began to relax, and soon I was asleep.

```
┌─────────────────────────────────┐
│                1                │
│                                 │
│              Elena              │
│                                 │
└─────────────────────────────────┘
```

ONE WEEK LATER...

Noah: *Breakfast? After you visit your mom, of course.*

I smiled at the text from Noah and stuffed my phone back into the pocket of my scrubs. I had ten more minutes before my shift was over, and then I could respond to him.

"Elena isn't your shift over soon," the charge nurse asked. I looked up from the paperwork I was filling out to respond.

"Yea, I have a few more patient files to complete, and then I'll be out of here." Julie nodded and then walked away. I saved my eye roll for when she was out of eyesight. I couldn't stand the lady, but I loved my job, so I dealt with it.

"She's such a buzz kill," Yasmine whispered from beside me. "I wish she'd go home. Things run so much smoother when she isn't here." I laughed but chose to keep my comments to myself. I wasn't one to engage in gossip with my co-workers because if shit were to hit the fan, they wouldn't waste any time throwing me under the bus to save their jobs. "Anyway, how are you liking New York so far?" Now that was a question I didn't mind answering.

"I love it," I chimed, flipping through the last of my paperwork and then setting it aside. "Coming here was one of the best decisions I ever made." It was true. I'd spent so much of my life taking care of my mother and not myself. When my brother suggested that we relocate, I'd already had it in my mind to make the move. I needed a change of scenery, and knowing that my mother was well taken care of made the transition much easier for me.

"That's great," she said. "If I had the guts, I'd leave New York and start over somewhere different."

"Why don't you?" I asked. "Have the guts that is?" She shrugged.

"I've been here my whole life; it's all I really know."

"That's a weak excuse." She looked at me with wide eyes, and I shrugged. "I lived in Michigan all my life. I even went to college there. And when my mother was diagnosed with Alzheimer's, I took over as her caregiver. Even still, when this opportunity came, I took it with no problem. You want to know that difference between you and me?" She nodded, eyes still a little wide by my bluntness. "You don't have anything holding you back. No children. No husband. No sick parent. You can do whatever you please. I wouldn't take that for granted."

"W-what happened to your mom?" I smiled at the thought of my ride or die. Sick or not, she was my everything.

"I brought her with me." I glanced at the time and then stood from my chair. "It's time for me to head out. Have a good shift." And with that, I walked away.

After grabbing my things, I headed out to Nova's car that was parked in the hospital parking lot. She rarely uses it and offered it to me since she mostly works from home or takes the train. Now that she's pregnant, I'm sure she'll want it back soon. My brother will never go for her taking the train while carrying his child. I slipped into the sleek Benz truck and pulled out my phone the second I was settled in my seat so that I could reply to Noah's text.

Me: *Are you cooking?*

His reply was quick.

Noah: *Whatever you want.*

I shot off a text of everything I wanted and then headed into the direction of the facility my mother lived in. I mentally prepared myself for her to not recognize me. There were days where she did, and days where she just stared at me in complete confusion. It hurt, but it was something I had to deal with. I refused to stop visiting to spare my feelings. I could never be that selfish. When my phone began to ring, I knew who it was without having to look at the screen. I answered and waited for the auto-mated system to finish its spiel. My father's deep voice blared through the speaker.

"...*Samuel Brooks.*"

I accepted the call and waited for us to be connected.

"Hey, baby girl." I smiled.

"Hey, dad," I said. "How are you?" My father was currently locked up for a murder I knew he didn't commit. No one thinks I know the truth, and I preferred to keep it that way. The less they think I know, the better.

"I'm as good as I can be. All things considered." There was a slight pause, and then he continued. "Are you headed to see your mother?"

"I am." He sighed deeply, and my heart broke a little for him. "If she remembers... tell her I love her."

"I tell her even when she doesn't."

"Thank you, baby girl."

"No need to thank me, dad."

"I—"

"When can I come see you?" It was a question I've been asking for years. He refuses to let me step foot in the federal prison he's being held at. I don't understand why, and he won't explain. There's a lot of things he won't explain. Like why he and Elijah are on bad terms. Everyone thinks they're protecting me from something, but they couldn't be more wrong.

"We've talked about this."

"We haven't actually," I quipped. "You just say it's for my own good, but you never give me an explanation. Elijah comes to see you."

"Barely."

"And I wonder why that is."

"Because he's stubborn." I chuckled. He had some nerve.

"I think it's because you're stuck in your ways. Nothing has changed in all the years you've been locked up." I paused as I whipped Nova's truck into the parking lot of the assisted living building. After finding a parking spot, I continued. "In those years, Elijah and I have changed. We've went from teenagers to adults with real life things going on. Your son just got married. He's about to be a father. And no matter what he says, he needs you. I need you." A heavy silence fell between us. I thought he would respond to what I said, but instead, I got a heavy sigh before the automated system warned us of our time almost being up.

"I love you, baby girl," he murmured into the phone.

"Yea, I love you too, dad." A few seconds later, the call ended, and I was heading inside to see my mother.

"Ms. Brooks," the front desk receptionist called out as I

entered the building. "Good to see you again. Your mother's nurse just headed into her room."

"Oh great," I said, smiling. "I always seem to miss her." I walked up the first-floor hall until I reached my mother's private apartment and pushed my way inside.

"Nurse Janay," I greeted. She looked up from her laptop and smiled.

"Hey, Elena. I was just finishing up. I didn't need much today, and she'd already been given her medication." I glanced at my mother, who was staring at me in deep confusion. I sighed and sat on the couch in her living room.

"Hey, mama."

"You've been quiet since you got here," Noah pointed out as he slid a plate filled with eggs, bacon, and pancakes. Next, he slid over a bowl of fruit and a cup of orange juice. "Do you want to talk about it?" Not meeting his gaze, I shrugged.

"Same ole, same ole."

"She didn't recognize you this time." I shook my head and tried my best not to cry. It didn't work. When Noah placed his arms around me, I broke down. Seeing her like that never got easy for me. If anything, the pain seemed more intense than before. "It'll be alright, Na. Don't cry." I shook in his arms. "I hate it when you cry."

"I'm sorry," I choked out.

"Don't be." He pulled me in closer. "I got you."

"T-thank you." Noah has been my rock through all of this. The moment we met almost eight months ago, I knew we'd become fast friends. I didn't plan on falling in love with him in the process, but he made it so easy. After calming down, I pulled away from him. I didn't want to look him in the eye, but he wasn't having it. Noah grabbed my chin and turned my head to face him. I lifted my gaze to meet his, and once again, he was staring at me with an unreadable expression on his face.

"Do you trust me?" he asked.

"Yes." I needed no time to think that question over.

"Alright, then hang with me for the rest of the day and let me make you feel better."

"I've been up for almost eighteen hours and—"

"Excuses," he said, cutting me off. "You can sleep here, and when you wake up, I'll take you somewhere, or we can chill here and binge something on tv." I smiled.

"Can we watch Degrassi?" He groaned, and I broadened my smile.

"If it'll make you feel better than yea, we can watch Degrassi." After jumping into his arms to thank him, he pushed me down into my seat and handed me a fork. "Eat."

"Aren't you going to eat with me?" I asked before stuffing a forkful of cheese eggs into my mouth.

"I'm grabbing me a plate now." I nodded and continued to scarf down my food. Noah was a great cook, and he insisted on making my meals as much as I'll allow. It all started six months ago, and I haven't been able to get rid of him since.

"Hello?" I answered after squinting at the unknown number.

"Elena?" My heart rate picked up. His voice was so distinctive.

"Noah?"

"Yea," he said, chuckling.

"How'd you get my number?" I hadn't talked to him since visiting New York the month prior.

"I stole it from Nova's phone." I bit down on my bottom lip to stop myself from laughing.

"Why would you do that?"

"Because she wouldn't have given it to me willingly, and I didn't feel like giving up a lung for it. Though I probably would have agreed to that if necessary." That time I let my laugh slip.

"Alright, well, to what do I owe this call?"

"I was wondering if I could make you breakfast."

"I— Why would you want to do that?" He chuckled, and I shifted in bed.

"You ask a lot of questions, Na."

"Na?"

"See more questions," he said. "How about you let me make you breakfast without asking me why this time?" It didn't take long for me to agree.

"OK."

"See how easy that was," he joked. "I'll pick you up in an hour. Is that enough time?"

"Y-yea."

"Cool."

He had ended the call that day as if it were nothing and true to his word, he was outside of Elijah's building an hour later. We've been inseparable since.

"What are you over there thinking about?" I looked up from my empty plate to meet his curious gaze. It was becoming harder and harder to look into his eyes and not want to blurt out how I felt. There were times where I swore, he was getting ready to tell me he felt more for me too.

"Nothing important," I said. "Can I have your bed?" I knew he didn't believe me, but I was grateful that he didn't push for more.

"You know you don't have to ask, Na." He stood and grabbed my plate. "There's some clean shirts in the basket on the floor too. I'm going to step out for a minute, but I'll be back before you wake up." I nodded. I slid out of my seat and headed toward his bedroom. After slipping out of my scrubs and into one of his shirts, I climbed into the massive bed that smelled just like him and buried myself beneath the blanket. The second my head hit the soft mound of pillows, I was out.

2

Noah

SHE WAS BEAUTIFUL.

Her hair was tangled and wild and covering most of her face.

A beautiful mess.

I leaned in the doorway of my bedroom while watching Elena sleep. When I'd left her two hours ago, she was so deep beneath the covers that I couldn't see her at all. And now she was all over the place. One leg and arm hung off the bed while the rest of her body was tangled in the sheets. The blanket was on the floor on the other side of the bed. She only slept wild when she was extremely tired. I hated it when she was this tired. If I weren't around, she'd sleep the whole day away and not get in a decent meal. I checked my watch and noted that it was still early afternoon. As bad as I wanted to wake her so I could see her beautiful eyes, I couldn't do it. I took her in one more time and then headed toward the kitchen to start dinner.

"Wassup, Nov?" I said after answering my vibrating phone.

"Hey, have you talked to Elena?" she asked, sounding concerned. "I went by the apartment, but she isn't there, and she isn't answering her phone."

"She's asleep in my bed."

"I— Oh, okay." There was a brief silence that passed, and then she started talking again. "I know I said I wouldn't get involved with whatever you two had going on, but Noah… you have to know that she—"

"Please don't say it," I pleaded. I couldn't hear what I already knew being said out loud. I wasn't ready to hear it. Not now, and I can't even be sure when.

"I see," Nova murmured. "I'm going to give you a bit of advice womb mate, and it'll be simple. Don't let her slip away because of fear. Fear is an ugly feeling, and it'll only hold you back." She ended the call, and I leaned up against the island in my kitchen while contemplating her words. I knew my sister was right. I knew that keeping how I felt about Elena from her would only push her away eventually. The thought alone had my chest tightening, so I can only imagine what it would feel like if it were to actually happen. Elena came into my life at a time where I didn't know I needed a friend.

"Do you always make breakfast for women you don't know," Elena *asked as she ran her hand over the marble island counter in my kitchen. I took in her lax state and smiled. She was mad beautiful and more comfortable then I'd thought she'd be.*

"I don't," I replied. "This is new for me."

She eyed me curiously and then asked, "How so?"

I didn't want to talk about my ex, but the words came tumbling out regardless.

"I'm newly single." She nodded and looked away from me. "We were together for fourteen years." Her wide eyes found me again. There was a hint of understanding in them too.

"I see," she started. "Young love that fizzled out?"

"On her end." I shrugged.

"Oh. So you still love her."

"I can't answer that because I'm not sure what it is that I feel right now. All I know is that I'm starting over, and it feels weird."

"Feels like maybe you don't know yourself anymore."

"Yea, do you know the feeling?" She nodded and took a seat in one of the bar stools.

"Not because of a relationship, but I've been feeling weird since moving here. I'm used to being on a tight schedule when it comes to the care of my mom, and now that she's not under my care anymore, I feel a little lost. Maybe you just need a friend."

"Maybe we both do." She smiled, and it damn near took my breath away. "So, friends?"

"Yea, friends."

Had I known that she would become so important to me in such a short time, I would have never allowed us to get so close. After things ended with Corrie—my ex—I had sworn off love. In my mind, us splitting was God's way of telling me that I wasn't built for long-lasting relationships. How could I be if Corrie wanted to end things after being together for so long? She was my everything. The most beautiful woman I think I'd ever laid eyes on until Elena. She changed it all for me, and now I'm confused.

Taking a deep breath, I stuck the pan of honey glazed salmon that I'd been working on into the oven and then prepped the veggies that will go along with it. After I finished with that, I went into the living room to find the DVD's that Elena raved about finding. She was obsessed with the show Degrassi but not the current one that airs on Netflix. She likes the old school one, and when she saw the DVD set in some store, I went out and bought it for her. Now I'm being subjected to watch it, but if I were being honest, then I really didn't mind.

"Noah?" Her sleep filled voice stilled me. It always did. I slowly turned to face her and took her in.

"You alright?" She nodded and pulled my shirt down further on her body. "Did you sleep good?"

"I always sleep good in your bed," she whispered, looking everywhere but at me. I reached out for her, and when her eyes found me again, she stepped closer and then into my arms. "Thank you."

"For?"

"Letting me sleep. I know how you'd rather me be awake so you can take care of me."

Laughing, I said, "Stop acting like you know me, Na." She leaned back a little to look up at me. Her mesmerizing eyes danced across my face.

"I know you well enough."

"Yea?"

"Mmhm." I wanted to ask what she meant by that, but she removed herself from my arms and walked toward the kitchen. I couldn't help but admire how amazing she looked in my shirt. Elena was short and petite. I wasn't a big guy, but compared to her, I was built like Dewayne Johnson. She was drowning in my shirt, and I liked the sight of it.

"Are you cooking?"

"Yea." I could still see her from where I was standing. She opened the oven and peeked inside then glanced my way with a broad smile on her face.

"My favorite." I nodded. "What's the occasion?" I tilted my head at her.

"Does there have to be one?"

"I don't know," she said, leaning against the sink. "I guess no one has ever done things for me just because." Her statement reminded me that we were still getting to know each other. And that no matter how long it felt like I knew her, she was still a mystery to me.

"I'm not everyone, Na."

"Yea, I've figured that out," she said, crossing her arms. "Did you do things like this for Corrie?"

"Where'd that question come from?" I asked, walking toward her. I didn't like the distance that she'd put between us. She did it more often than not.

"I guess I'm just curious about who you were to her. How you were with her." She shrugged. "I wonder if you were the same with her as you are with me." I rubbed a hand down my face and looked away from her.

"Na... you know I hate talking about her."

"I know... I— Never mind. I'm sorry."

"Don't be sorry for being curious." I walked closer and blocked her in. "I just want to leave the past in the past. She's no longer a part of my life, and I want it to stay that way."

"But she was once a big part of your life, and I just want to know everything about you, but I understand." I decided to be honest with her.

"It's something that I'm still confused about." A flash of something flickered in her eyes, but it was gone too soon for me to catch what it was.

"I get it. We don't have to talk about it." She sounded disappointed, and I hated that. I never want to be the reason she's disappointed about something. "Can we start watching Degrassi while we wait for dinner?"

Sighing, I nodded and said, "Dinner is for later. Let's make lunch, and then we can start." She nodded and slipped past me. I kept my attention on the faucet in front of me. I'd just fucked up somehow, and I wasn't sure how.

"Noah... Lunch."

"Right. Let's get to it."

"I DON'T GET IT. Your brother had a great season, and the team still sucked," Loke said, slashing a hand through the air. I chuckled and then sipped on my beer. Samir glared at him, and I laughed harder.

"That was more of a compliment," I said. "The team sucked, but your brother by himself had a damn good season." Samir's brother played for the New York Giants. He was the teams saving grace at the beginning of the season. It gave us all hope, but eventually, that little bit of hope fizzled out. They didn't make it out of the first round of the playoffs, and it had the fans really angry. As usual. "There's only so much a running back can do," I added.

"When he gets here, let's not talk about the season." Loke gave a noncommittal grunt, and I shook my head. Samir had invited us out tonight so that we could get his brother's mind off not only missing out on the Super Bowl but also his injury that happened the last game of the Giants season. It could possibly have him out for at least half of the upcoming season.

"Should he even be out on his leg?" Elijah asked, tossing his head toward the door. I turned to see that Semaj had entered and was walking on his leg without the crutch I know he should have.

"This dummy," Samir grumbled, standing to meet him.

"Aye, Noah, you good?" Elijah asked, gaining my attention.

"Yea, what made you ask that?" He eyed me curiously before answering my question.

"You seem off."

"Nah. I'm good. You can report that back to my nosy ass twin."

He nodded and asked, "And is my sister good?"

"As far as I know, she is." He gave me a hard look and then nodded. I came out tonight at her insistence. I would have preferred chilling with her at my place or hers. When I wasn't traveling for work, all I wanted was to be with her. I had a feeling she wanted the night to herself. Away from me. I tuned out the conversation happening around me and pulled my phone out of my pocket.

Me: *Are you enjoying your night?*

Elena: *Aren't you supposed to be drinking beer and having guy talk right now?*

Me: *Yea, but I wanted to check on you.*

Elena: *I'm fine. I have a glass a wine in my hand, and I'm about to dive into a new book.*

Elena: *Enjoy your night.*

Damn.

She'd just dismissed me. I stuffed my phone back into my pocket and brought my attention back to the table.

"How about you get out there on that field and take a team to the Super Bowl," Semaj seethed, glaring at Loke.

"Your quarterback sucks," Loke said nonchalantly with a smirk on his face. He was enjoying fucking with him. Semaj opened his mouth and then shut it.

"You know what… off the record, he does suck." He picked up his beer and took a long swig. "And the idiot won't admit that it's time for him to retire. He's just one of those guys that want to play until he's sixty. The front office won't admit it either."

"Why not throw some weight around?" I asked. He looked my way and dropped his shoulders.

"I don't want a bad locker room experience."

"But maybe they need your leadership."

"Leadership?"

"You aren't a rookie anymore. You've proven yourself

to be an asset." I took another sip of my beer. "I'm not saying step on any toes, but I am saying that you have the power to sway some of the votes on what should happen. Make some light-hearted suggestions for the future and see where that gets you." He gave another thoughtful look my way and then nodded. I wasn't fully aware of sports politics, but I knew how to sway someone in favor of me. As the conversation around the table changed, thoughts of Elena filled my mind. I wanted her for myself, but I refused to hurt her. I would never allow myself to do that, especially when I knew that my current state of mind wasn't the best for a new relationship. I'm just not sure how much longer I can keep up this whole, *'we're just friends'* charade.

```
┌─────────────────────────────────────┐
│                                     │
│                 3                   │
│                                     │
│              Elena                  │
│                                     │
└─────────────────────────────────────┘
```

"I NEVER THOUGHT I'D FALL IN LOVE THIS WAY," I murmured, glancing at my mom. "I mean he's an amazing guy. He's handsome, with a good job, an amazing family, and he's so respectful. I just…" I paused and turned to face her completely. She was focused on knitting and not paying me any attention. At least I thought…

"I think you should tell this friend of yours how you feel," she said, smiling at me. "Sometimes, they need a little push."

"I'm afraid if I do that, I'll be pushing too hard, and I'll lose him altogether."

"Maybe you need to lose him for him to see that he doesn't want to lose you."

"Mama—"

"Who?" she asked, squinting at me. I knew she didn't recognize who I was, but it did feel good to have her talking to me like we were old friends. I sighed and turned back toward the window. "If you love him, you'll do whatever it takes to get him, and if he doesn't see that you're a great catch, then he doesn't deserve you."

"Even if it'll hurt?"

"Even then." I tapped the window seal while trying to get my thoughts together. Telling him how I felt will be easier said than done. "You said this friendship is still new, right?" I turned to her and nodded.

"A little under a year.

"Well then, don't rush it. You don't have to tell him everything right now. Enjoy his company. Learn more about him, and then when the time is right, just go for it."

"How will I know when the time is right?"

"When you aren't asking yourself if it's the right time." She smiled at me and then continued to knit away.

Ok, Elena. Just go with the flow. You can do that.

A few hours later, I was clocking in for my night shift at the hospital.

"Glad to see you're on shift tonight, Elena," Doctor Joseph said, walking up beside me. I continued flipping through my patient charts for the night. I was working in the emergency room tonight, and hopefully, it stayed quiet throughout my twelve-hour shift.

"Glad to be here," I finally answered, giving him my attention. Doctor Randall Joseph has tried asking me out more than once since I started here, and I have turned him down each time. It wasn't that he wasn't good looking or even charming, but he just wasn't the man for me.

He smiled, showing off his deep dimples and said, "Maybe we could eat lunch together." I shook my head.

"Randall—"

"Nothing like that. Just two co-workers eating lunch together in the cafeteria." I eyed him skeptically, and he threw his hands up. "I swear I don't have a hidden agenda." He definitely had a hidden agenda, but instead of calling him out on it, I picked up a chart and got to work.

"If you see me in there, then sure, and if not, then

maybe you'll catch me another time." He nodded and walked away. The second he was out of earshot, Yasmine —who was also working tonight—leaned over the nurse's station and shook her head.

"I don't see how you keep turning that man down." She bit down on her bottom lip. "He is a beautiful specimen."

"He's not my type," I said, laughing. She gave me a weary look and then sat down.

"I'm afraid to ask what your type is then." I smiled and pulled my phone out. I wasn't one to give away too much of my personal life to my co-workers, but I felt like showing off a little. I walked around to the other side of the nurse's station and sat down next to Yasmine. I scrolled through the gallery on my phone until I reached the picture that Noah and I took together at Nova and Elijah's wedding a few weeks back. Yasmine leaned into the phone after I held it out to her.

"Wow," she whispered. "Is that your boyfriend?"

"My best friend," I said. She looked up at me and then back at the picture.

"You guys look like you're more than just friends. Look at how he's staring at you." I glanced at the picture and forced myself to not swoon. "And Jesus, he is handsome." That he was.

"I take it he's your type." I nodded, locked my phone, and then stuck it back in my scrubs pocket.

"He's definitely got something on the doc." She tapped on the computer keys in front of her and then turned in her seat. "Can I ask you something?"

"Sure."

"I guess it's not really a question. I was asked out by someone, and I'm not sure how to take it."

"What do you mean?"

"Well, he was dating this girl that's like an artist or whatever, and she kind of broke up with him a while back. He was broken up about it, and he confided in me. We've been kind of close since then, and recently he asked me out. I just… I don't know. He told me she's pregnant and recently got married. I don't want to be his rebound, but I do really like him." I stared at her for a second before responding.

"Who's the guy?" I had an idea, but I wanted to be sure.

"Liam Colston."

"The doctor?" She nodded and bit down on her lip. I laughed. I didn't mean to, but I couldn't help myself. Liam was Nova's ex. Yasmine had just explained my friend's life and didn't know she was talking to her friend, let alone her sister-in-law.

"And she's beautiful, Elena. I saw pictures on his phone before he deleted them all."

"Yea?"

"Yea… any advice?" I shrugged.

"I say go out with him. I think he's over her." Liam was definitely over Nova and had even been at the wedding. He wanted to see her happy, and now that she is, I think he's finally ready to move on. I just had no idea Yasmine would be the girl.

"Wait… how would you know?" I chuckled and showed her another picture. It was of Nova and Noah. "Hey! That's her." She squinted at the image and then looked up at me. "That's your best friend."

"Mmhm, and that is his twin sister, and she's married to my brother." Her eyes widened, and she covered her mouth.

"Shit," she grumbled. "This is embarrassing. I had no idea."

"Don't sweat it. You didn't say anything bad, Yas." I shrugged and tucked my phone away once again. "I think you should take him up on the offer and see for yourself if he's over her or not." She smiled and nodded.

"I think I will."

"Good," I said. "I need to start my rounds, and those will take a little while. If you need me, page me."

"CAN I ASK YOU SOMETHING?" Noah murmured into the phone. I glanced around the cafeteria and then back at the slice of pizza in front of me. I was on my lunch break, spending it as I always do, which was on the phone with Noah if he was available to talk.

"Sure," I said, picking off a pepperoni and popping it into my mouth.

"You know what…" he paused, and I furrowed my eyebrows. "Never mind. Are you actually eating, or are you picking at your food as usual." *That's odd.* Even though I wanted to know what that was about, I chose to go with the flow instead of calling him out.

"You don't know me," I joked, lifting my eyes to see Doctor Joseph heading my way. I held back the eye roll that wanted so desperately to escape and focused my attention on my pizza.

"I know you very well, Na."

"Nurse Brooks," Doctor Joseph greeted, helping himself to the seat across from me.

"Who is that?" Noah asked.

"Doctor Joseph, I'm kind of on the phone," I pointed out, removing the device from my ear to show him before placing it back just in time to hear Noah ask once again who I was talking to.

"You said—"

"I know what I said, but I'm not available right now." I stared at him pointedly. "Actually I need some air, excuse me." I stood from my seat while also gathering my trash with my free hand. I dumped it on the way out of the cafeteria.

"Na?"

"Yes, Noah?"

"You sound annoyed." I stepped out into the brisk night and took a gulp of cool air into my lungs.

"That's because I am a little annoyed," I admitted. For some reason, I hated being interrupted when I was talking to Noah. I can deal with family or even friends being the one to do it, but it was something about Randall freaking Joseph sliding into the chair across from me while I was on the phone with Noah that irked me.

"Why?"

"I—" I quickly stopped myself from explaining. I wasn't trying to sound crazy, and I felt this may have one thing that he wouldn't understand. "Just ready to get off work and get some sleep." It wasn't a complete lie.

"Ok," he mumbled, not believing a thing I said. I could hear it in his tone. "Who was the guy?"

"One of the doctors on staff... he's got this thing for me." I pressed my back up against the cold brick and sighed.

"Is that right?"

"Yea, he's been trying since I started, and it's becoming annoying."

"So, you don't want to take him up on his offer?"

"No, why would I?" I could hear the disgust in my own voice.

"You're single... why wouldn't you?" I had a response to that, but I decided not to give it. Noah was poking at something that he obviously wasn't ready to hear and quite frankly something I'm not prepared to say.

"It doesn't matter," I said, waving my hand dismissively as if he could see it. "Noah, my lunch is about over, and I need to get back. I'll talk to you in the morning."

"Alright," he said. "Aye, Na?" he called out before I could hang up.

"Yes?"

"I love you." I stopped walking and bit down on my lip. He sounded different. The words sounded different this time, and I wasn't sure what to make of it.

Instead of asking questions that I probably wouldn't get the answers to tonight, I responded with, "I love you too, Noah." I was sure that things had shifted somehow between us, and that thought alone scared me. I shook away my thoughts and headed back toward the ER. I had eight hours left in my shift, and my attention needed to be solely on that. As I passed the cafeteria, I rolled my eyes.

Just my luck, I thought as Doctor Joseph came walking out. He looked up from his phone and smiled.

"Elena."

"Randall," I replied.

"Sorry about the whole interrupting your call thing, won't happen again."

"Appreciate that," I said after looking him over and seeing nothing but sincerity in his eyes. I honestly think that he's just used to getting his way with the ladies, and that's why I intrigue him so much. Randall was a handsome man, and maybe in another life where I wasn't already hung up on someone, I would have given him a legit chance. I shook my head. Yea, probably not. He opened his mouth to speak, but both of our pagers went off. I looked down at it and, with wide eyes, took off running toward the ER.

Code Green.

An external disaster had taken place, and that meant we were about to be bombarded with a slew of injured people. I'd had my share of these while living in Michigan, but this would be my first as a New York nurse. Tonight just got interesting…

I pushed my way through the doors and ran right into Yasmine.

"Oh my God, Elena!" she screeched eyes wide. "There you are."

"What's happening?" I looked around while she explained.

"Some type of explosion in Tribeca. We don't have the details just that we have about six ambulances headed this way with severely injured people." I nodded and moved around her.

"Brooks, outside with me," the charge nurse instructed on her way past me. I grabbed a pair of gloves and followed her out. "I hope you're ready because these things never end well for a lot of people. Keep your head clear and move fast." I gave her a look that said, *I'm not new to this,* and turned at the sound of an ambulance shrill in the distance. *Time to save some lives.*

4

Noah

"How have you been, sweetie," my mother asked, handing me a bottle of water. "Any new business trips coming up?" I took my time popping the cap on the chilled bottle and then gulped down half of it. Afterward, I twisted the cap back on and then leaned back in my seat.

"I leave for Arizona in a couple of days. I have a potential new client out there." She nodded and sipped on her tea. As an art gallery dealer, I bought and sold paintings all over the world. My job was one that I loved, and because of it, I've experienced parts of the world that people rarely get to see. I knew there was something else on my mother's mind. She hadn't asked me over here to question me about something that she could have called about.

"You didn't answer my first question," she pointed out, narrowing her dark brown eyes at me.

"I'm fine old lady."

"You and your sister will get enough of calling me old," she fussed. "I'm as fine as I was back in the day." I chuckled and shook my head. She was right. She didn't look a day over thirty, but calling her old was one of my favorite past times. "I've been worried about you." Her wide smile slowly drifted away and was replaced with a more serious look. A motherly one.

"There's nothing for you to be worried about."

"Oh, but there is." I tilted my head at her. I knew what this was about. "Since Corrie left, you haven't been yourself." I tapped on the table and kept my gaze away from hers. I knew that eventually, the conversation of Corrie would come up. She'd given me close to nine months, and that was longer than I'd anticipated. "Well, that is until recently."

"What do you mean?" I asked, placing my eyes on hers. She shrugged and sipped her tea.

"You seem content."

Elena.

I was content, and she was the reason for that. Elena made me see reason, but that didn't stop me from wanting to not take things too far. My contentment was based on our friendship. It was all I was worthy of when it came to her.

"I'm getting through." I gulped down the rest of my water and stood to throw the bottle away.

"Corrie called me," she said, cutting into the silence. "She wanted to know how you were. She said that you weren't taking her calls."

"And what did you tell her?" I asked, turning to face her. She had a deep frown on her face, and it mirrored Nova more than usual.

"That it wasn't my business to pass your business along." I nodded and leaned against the counter.

"She lied to you," I started, pausing to let out a strangled laugh. I found none of this funny, but it was the only thing that was keeping me calm. "She hasn't called since she left." I didn't appreciate her trying to use my mother for information when she can easily pick up the phone and call me herself. Corrie wasn't stupid. She was one of the smartest women I know. It was what attracted me to her in the beginning. Her looks are what made me approach her, but after that first conversation… it was her brains. She drew me in, and I was stuck there for fourteen years. A waste of time, and I can never get that time back. And maybe I'm a little bitter that the woman I wanted to marry decided that the life we'd built wasn't good enough anymore. That *I* wasn't good enough anymore. Her last words before she walked out of the apartment, we once shared plays in my mind more often then I'd like.

"I'm sorry, Noah," she cried, stepping away from me. "I know this is not what we planned, but I need to let you go for me. I need to see what else is out there."

She needed to see what else was out there. I still haven't figured out if she meant that she wants to explore her options when it comes to men. Or maybe I have figured it out.

"Can I ask you something, ma?" I looked up to find her watching me intently. She responded with no words but a slight nod. "When does it stop hurting?" As soon as the words left my mouth, my eyes began to burn.

Fuck.

I didn't come here for this. I didn't want to feel. I wanted to move the fuck on.

"When you allow it," she murmured, pulling me into her arms. "Allow yourself to let go." I was getting there, but it didn't mean the shit would hurt any less.

"Wassup, sis." Her voice was low as she responded.

"Hey, twin," she said. "Are you okay? I've been getting

not so great vibes all day, and I know it's you." I chuckled. Of course, she felt my energy. I've been in a weird mood since leaving my mom's earlier. Being a twin had its perks. For Nova and me, we could feel what the other was feeling but kind of heightened. I never feel when she's in pain, only when she's extremely excited. But she can feel my agony and sadness. Most people find that little tidbit intriguing, and then they launch into a million questions after finding out. It's the main reason we don't talk about it much.

"My day hasn't been that great," I admitted. If I could talk to anyone about this, it was Nova. I pulled my truck into the parking lot of the Presbyterian Hospital and parked. Nova's sigh flowed through my car speakers.

"It's about Corrie, isn't it?"

"You read minds now?"

No, but I know it isn't about your precious Elena."

"Corrie called mom and lied about reaching out to me," I said, ignoring her comment about Elena. She didn't want to interfere with us, and that meant in all aspects for me. "She was fishing for information, but I'm confused about why she didn't call herself."

"That's easy," she said, laughing. "She doesn't want to talk, but she wants to keep tabs. Basically, she's wondering if you've moved on yet, but she didn't want to know bad enough to call you herself and see. Corrie knows not to call me, so she went to the next best person."

"She was better off trying pop." Nova's infectious laugh filled my truck, and it made me smile.

"True that," she said. "Dad is a sucker for keeping the peace." After a brief silence, she added, "She doesn't deserve you."

"What if I was the one who didn't deserve her?"

"Bullshit!" I could hear the anger in her tone. "You

were nothing but good to her ungrateful ass. She wanted to explore her options, and now she's doing that. If I wasn't pregnant, I'd be on the next flight to Oxford."

"It's never that serious. Keep my niece or nephew safe from stress."

"I'm doing that," she whined. "I just hate that you're suffering because of her. I want you to be happy."

"Me too," I mumbled, watching Elena walk out of the hospital with a bright smile on her beautiful face. She spotted my truck and headed my way.

"I think you've found happiness." She paused and then said, "Don't let her slip away."

"I have to go." I ended the call and hopped out.

"What are you doing here?" Elena asked, smile brighter than before.

"I came to pick you up."

You didn't have to do that, Noah," she fussed. "I was going to take an Uber."

"Yea, but I'm leaving tonight, and I'll be gone for two weeks. I wanted to see you." I opened the passenger side door for her, and she slipped inside. After closing her in, I made my way around the truck and then settled back into my seat.

"I thought you weren't leaving for a few days." I shrugged and pulled out onto the road, heading into the direction of her apartment. Once Nova and Elijah moved in together, he gave her his place.

"I got a lead on an art show that's happening tomorrow night, and I wanted to catch it." The truth was I'd been known about the art show, and I planned on skipping it, but the idea of getting away earlier than usual was appealing. And after the visit with my mother, I decided leaving early was a good idea.

"And you wanted to see me before you left," she mused.

"I feel special." I cut an eye at her and caught the beautiful smile she was still sporting.

"You have no idea how special you are to me."

"Noah, are you okay?"

"I am now." And I meant that. I pulled into the parking lot of her building, placed my truck in park, and then turned in my seat. "How was your shift? What happened that you had to stay over so late?" She was usually off at seven, but she'd texted me earlier this morning saying she wouldn't be off until about eleven.

"There was some explosion in Tribeca, and we were flooded. It was intense, but we had no casualties." There was that bright smile again.

"I love that you love your job."

"It makes me happy," she whispered. "Saving lives."

"I was thinking…" She licked her lips, and my words got caught in my throat.

"You were thinking…" I shook my head and laughed.

"Do you think you could get a couple of days off and meet me in Arizona?" Asking her hadn't been a part of the plan until just now.

"I—really?" I shrugged. I was trying to play it cool, but I really wanted her to come.

"Yes, really." She nodded and looked away from me. Elena was shy at times. I realized it right from the start. The thing is, she's also bold. She was the perfect mixture of… perfection.

"Okay," she murmured. "Yea, I can see if I'm able to get some time off." I watched her fumble with the strap of her bookbag, and I wanted to ask what was on her mind, but now wasn't the time.

"Get inside and get some sleep," I ordered. "And make sure you eat, Elena. No picking at your food."

"My father's in jail, Noah White." She turned to face me with a frown on her face. "Stop telling me what to do."

"I like bossing you around." She chuckled and opened her door. After slipping out, she leaned in to grab her bag. She took one last look at me and shook her head.

"I kind of like you bossing me around too." And with that, she shut the door and sashayed into her building. Before pulling off, I grabbed my phone and shot off a quick text to her.

Me: *If you get the time off, don't think about spending a dime of your money on getting to me. I'll take care of everything.*

She sent back the middle finger emoji, and it made me smile.

Shy but bold.

Deep down, I knew I was contradicting everything I said before. I didn't want to hurt her, and I didn't feel ready to explore more, but the constant reminder from Nova to not let her slip away has me wanting to try. What would be the harm in trying?

5

Elena

I STARED AT MY RINGING PHONE WHILE MUNCHING ON A handful of almonds. I'd decided a few days ago that purposely missing a couple of calls from my dad would convince him to let me come see him. It bothered me that he and Elijah called themselves protecting me. I didn't need protection. What I needed was my father, and visiting him is the best I'll ever get.

"Forcing his hand is smart," I mumbled.

"He won't budge," Elijah interjected from his spot across from me. I lifted my head to meet his eyes and then rolled them. "I'm telling you from experience."

"Yea well, I wouldn't know what your experience was since you never wanted to talk about it." I rolled my eyes again and stuffed more almonds into my mouth. I didn't want Elijah here with me, but he insisted on us hanging. Something about sibling time before Nova has the baby. A bunch of bullshit if you ask me. This was his way of getting information on Noah and me so he can report back to his wife. "So, if you aren't going to tell me about it, then please don't try to talk me out of what I'm doing."

"I won't," he agreed. "But take my advice, little sis. Pop is selfish. The only selfless thing he's ever done was…" his words trailed, and I stared at him, waiting for the bomb to drop, but it never came. "Just protect your heart."

"From dad or Noah?"

"Both."

"Now we're getting down to your real reason for being here." He peered at me, and I shrugged. "Go on. Speak your peace."

"Nova told me about your break down."

"Remind me to never confide in Nova again. I'll stick to talking to Brynlee." I knew calling Nova the day before New Year's in tears that it would get back to my brother. I didn't call her because Noah had done something wrong to me. I called because he was everything that's right in my life. Everything that I know he's not willing to give me. She mistook my tears for something else. "I don't need protecting from Noah. He would never hurt me."

"You sound sure."

"That's because I am, Elijah," I quipped. "I've never been so sure about something in my life." He threw his hands up in mock surrender and chuckled. It made me smile. Elijah has changed since Nova came into his life. The serious, no-nonsense, rarely smiling man I used to know has a spark to him now.

"I tried to tell Nova the same thing." His smile grew. "I know Noah won't hurt you. He cares too much." I eyed my big brother curiously, and he just shrugged my questioning look off. "Nova knows the same, but she's just worried about her brother."

"I'm worried too just not in the same way that Nova is." I grabbed two bottles of cran-apple juice from the fridge and slid one Elijah's way. "He'll be fine, though. I'm going to meet him in Arizona this weekend."

"Yea?" I nodded. "Good luck."

"Thanks." *But I don't think I'll need it.*

———

"WE'VE BEEN to every aisle in this store, and you still haven't found anything that you were supposedly looking for." Brynlee cut an eye at me and then continued to sift through the rack of fabric in front of her. We were supposed to be searching for the perfect color for her bridesmaids to wear. Though Brynlee and Samir were already married, they were still having a summer wedding. "Bryn—"

"I'm gaining weight, and it's driving me crazy. I don't need this right now. I need to be the same weight that I was before meeting Samir," she fussed, not making any sense. What did her weight have to do with fabric? I opted out of asking and looked her over with a frown on my face.

"You look the same," I pointed out. "Actually, you look like you've lost some weight." She was petite as ever but a nice height, so it didn't look bad. She looked damn good. I didn't understand where this extra weight was that she was talking about. "Bryn, what's going on with you?" She waved her hand dismissively and then turned to face me.

"Let's talk about you."

"Why does everyone keep wanting to talk to me about me?" I rolled my eyes and moved through the store. "No one wants to be involved, but it seems like no one can stop asking questions. I mean, what's up with that?" Brynlee fell into stride with me and then bumped my shoulder.

"Everyone is just… concerned, I guess."

"No, they aren't," I said. "You guys are just in love and happy, and you want to force that on Noah and me." She chuckled.

"Maybe… or we just see what you guys are forcing yourselves not to."

"What if we aren't forcing ourselves not to see what we have, then what?"

Brynlee stepped in front of me and gripped my shoulders.

"If that's not the case, then don't worry about what any of us think," she said. "I'll talk to them and try to get them off your case." I tilted my head at her, and she smiled.

"Why are you helping?" She shrugged and turned to walk out of the store. Once we were out in the parking lot and in front of Samir's car, she answered my question.

"Because I wasn't one of the people who said I didn't want parts in your… thing. I'm here for you if you need advice or to vent."

"Yea, I know." She'd reminded me of that at Elijah and Nova's wedding.

"Act like it then," she ordered. "Now that we have that out of the way let's go get ice cream."

"But didn't you just—"

"Please don't deny me." Brynlee poked her bottom lip out and then smiled quickly after that.

"Fine, let's go."

A few hours later, I was spread out in my bed, munching on a family-sized bag of spicy Doritos with more on my mind then I'd like. I was beginning to under-stand why Elijah felt the way he did about our father. He was a selfish man, and everything had to be done under his command. How he'd managed to still have control in this way from behind bars was beyond me.

At one point and time, my father was my hero. He was everything a little girl needed until he wasn't. When he went to jail, it broke me, but I pushed that pain back. I had to. It's what we women do. We take the brunt of the hurt, and then we fix everyone else around us while being left damaged beyond repair afterward. I felt damaged. Deep down, I know I'm not, but what I feel on the surface is painful. The vibrating of my phone pulled me from my thoughts, and the sight of Noah's name made me smile.

Noah: *Don't eat too many.*

I looked down at the giant bag of chips and laughed. How did he know?

Me: *Noah…*

Noah: *You eat more junk food than regular food, and your favorite is Doritos. I'm only guessing…*

Me: *You could be wrong.*

I popped a few chips into my mouth for good measure.

Noah: *But I'm not, though.*

Me: *Fine, but I did eat a regular meal today with Brynlee.*

My phone rang, and it was a facetime call from Noah. I wanted to jump up and check my face out in the mirror before answering but decided against it. He'd seen me at my worse already.

"Hey," I answered when his sweaty face came into view. "You were working out?"

"Yea, just a little cardio." He smiled. "Samir called me." I rolled my eyes.

"Oh, yea, about what?"

"Something about being there for me if I need to talk, and he thinks Brynlee might be pregnant."

"What!" I thought back to her complaining about gaining weight, and it was starting to make sense. I didn't see it, but she feels it. *Oh, my God.*

"Yea, but she's in denial or some shit. I don't know." I stared at Noah with a smirk on my face. I love how he tries to make gossiping with me, not sound like gossip, and he hates when I say that it is. "Don't start, Na."

"I wasn't even going to say anything."

"But you were thinking it," he quipped. "What time does your flight get in on Friday?"

"I sent you my itinerary."

"And I looked at it, but I'm still asking you." He wasn't looking at the camera as he spoke. The sound of liquid moving around let me know that he was shaking up his nasty protein drink.

"Noon," I answered.

"And you're here until…" His voice trailed, and then he glanced at the camera.

"Tuesday." He nodded and then put the shaker cup to his lips and downed the drink inside in the blink of an eye. A call coming through blocked out our facetime call, and I sighed.

"Why you got me paused?"

"I have a phone call coming through, and I'm letting it ring out."

"Who don't you want to talk to?" he asked as the call ended, and he came back into view.

"My dad."

"He still won't let you come see him?" I shrugged.

"I'm not sure if he changed his mind because I haven't been answering his calls. I need a break." A beat of silence passed between us before he spoke again.

"Can I ask you something?"

"Always…"

"Why haven't you told him or Elijah that you know the truth?" I had a feeling that's what he wanted to ask. I had confided in Noah one night about my father. The story that everyone knows isn't the truth and when I found out… I was shocked and confused, but I kept my mouth closed about it. My father was convicted of a murder that he didn't commit, but my mother did. He took the charge to save her from the life he's living, but sometimes I wonder if it's worth it because she isn't really living. She might not physically be behind bars, but mentally she is, and that's worse, in my opinion.

"Sometimes, I want to tell them, but then I don't see the point," I finally answered. "Elijah thinks he's protecting me, and I have no idea what my dad thinks, but I'd rather not open wounds that don't need opening."

"Are you okay with knowing?"

"That's a hard question to answer."

"Why?"

"Because I feel OK, but I don't know if I really am." Admitting that out loud felt good.

"You're strong, you know that?"

Here he goes…

Noah always said the sweetest things. The right things at the right time. I don't even think he knows that he's doing it. He just genuinely cares, and it shows through his actions but also his words.

"Yea, I know."

"Even if you didn't know, I'd remind you every day if need be."

"Yea?" He nodded and flashed his beautiful smile. "I appreciate you. This friendship is… thank you."

"Thank me by eating something today," he said, ruining the moment. "I have to go, but I'll see you Friday, alright?"

"Alright."

The facetime call ended, and I flopped back against the mass of pillows behind me. I wasn't sure if me going to spend the weekend with Noah was the right move, but I was doing it. My mother was right. I didn't need to move fast with him or reveal how I feel right away. I just pray it doesn't blow up in my face.

"YOU'RE BACK," TIM REED GREETED. HE WAS THE director of the art gallery I attended a couple of nights ago. When I walked into his space, he'd somehow known exactly who I was.

"I'm back." I glanced around the gallery and nodded. I liked how it looked during the day without a crowd of people. "There was a painting here by this artist." I pulled out his card and handed it to Tim. He glanced at it and then back at me.

"Ah. Jameson. Yes, he's popular here, but if you have his information, then what is it that I can do for you?"

I looked him over and then back around the gallery once again.

"I'd like you to be the go between," I said, placing my gaze back on him. His eyes widened, and I knew he was seeing dollar signs. I usually worked alone because I was just that good, but if I come across art that was displayed in a gallery than I always work with the director. And I always wait until after the event to purchase any work. Even if it's something that I know will sell before I get to it.

I've always felt that if it was meant for me, then it'll still be there, and the theory has worked over the years.

"I'll contact him for you," he said. "He's not in contract with us. He only brings paintings for shows and then takes them afterward. His father—"

"I know who he is," I said, cutting him off. Jameson Wright was well known. A simple google search gave me all the information I needed on him.

"Right," he murmured. "I'll go make that call. Take a look around while you wait, I won't be long."

As he walked away, I checked my watch and noted that I had an hour and a half to spare before I needed to start making my way to the airport. I figured I could get some business done before Elena arrived. I wanted to give her all of my attention this weekend, and that meant holding off on some work until she's gone. It would be worth it.

"Mr. White, Jameson wasn't available, but I was able to leave a message with his assistant," Tim said as he entered the gallery from the back. I pulled out my card and handed it to him.

"When you hear from him, you call me." I left the gallery and headed for my rental car. As soon as I was situated, I connected my phone to the car and then called Nova. She'd called me a few times this morning, but it was always at times where I was busy.

"Noah... I could've been dead," she whined.

"And yet here you are whining on my phone," I said, pulling onto the highway. "What do you need, sis?"

"Elena's coming there and—"

"You called to be in my business." She sighed, and I continued. "What happened to you not wanting any parts in this?"

"That was before I realized that she means more to you than just some fling."

"She was never a fling, Nov," I explained. "I've never even touched her in that way."

"Well, I know that now, and I want to help," she said. "You do want more, don't you?"

"I—I don't know if I can handle that," I admitted. "But yes, I want more."

"You don't give yourself enough credit. I know what happened with Corrie changed you a little, but maybe that was for the better. You said that maybe you wanted out of that situation and didn't realize it until after she proposed it, so what changed?"

"Nothing," I answered. I didn't plan on telling her that I felt unworthy, but I would reveal another fear. "It's just... Corrie was who I was used to. I don't know how to be with anyone else, and I don't want to fuck this up. I can't fuck up with her. Not *her*." Elena was special to me. Hurting her would kill me.

"I get it, but if you don't try, then you'll lose her."

"I am trying; that's why she's coming here." That part was true. Even with all of my fears, I still wanted to try.

"Does she know that?"

"No, and I don't plan on telling her. I don't want it to be awkward."

"Well, look... something is going on with her. I don't know if it's about her father or mother, but she's been different lately. Brynlee even noticed."

"Yea, I've noticed too, and she knows to come to me if she needs me."

"Well, I guess this call was pointless." She chuckled and then sighed. "When you get back, can we hang? I feel like I haven't seen much of you since the wedding."

"Movies and dinner?"

"That sounds nice, I'm down."

"I'm pulling up to the airport now to grab Elena," I said. "I'll call you later on, and Nov... thank you."

"Always. Later, womb mate."

I pulled my rental into an empty spot and then placed it in park. It wasn't as crowded as the day I'd got here, but it was still a lot of people and steady traffic. I checked the time and was satisfied to see that I was early. Elena's flight won't land for another ten minutes if it's on time. I checked the Delta website to get confirmation that it was, in fact, on time and then laid my head back with my eyes closed.

"Shit," I mumbled, snapping my eyes open at the sound of my phone. "Hello?"

"Noah, are you sleeping?" Elena asked. "Please don't tell me you're sleeping."

"I didn't realize I'd fallen asleep." I looked up to see that the white truck that was once sitting in front of me was long gone and replaced with a black Nissan. I was surprised that someone hadn't tapped on my window to ask me to move yet.

"So, you aren't here, then?"

"What? Oh... yea, I'm here. I'm in my car, where are you?"

"Waiting on my bags." Her voice sounded far away. "You must be tired if you're sleeping in your car."

"I had a long morning," I said, stepping out of my car and walking to the other side so that I could lean up against it. "I'm right in front of door four."

"OK, I'll be out as soon as they give up our bags." I stuck my phone in my pocket and crossed my arms. For reasons unknown, my heart had begun to beat faster than normal. Was I anxious to see her, or was it something else? There were too many thoughts running through my mind for me to pinpoint what was what at the moment.

"Noah..." Her voice was like music to my ears. I lifted

my head to find Elena walking toward me with a broad smile on her face. She had on a pair of oversized sunglasses that covered most of her face. "Wow. You really do look sleepy." Laughing, I approached her and took the bag she was carrying and suitcase from her. After popping the trunk and placing them inside, I turned and pulled her into my arms. I removed the sunglasses so that I could see her eyes.

"I missed you."

"Yea?" she whispered into my chest.

"Yea."

"I missed you too." I held onto her a little longer and then pulled away.

"Get in so we can get out of here. I'm sure they're watching me now. I've been sitting here longer than most."

"And sleeping," she pointed out before slipping into the passenger seat.

"Yea, that too," I agreed after situating myself back into my seat. I looked over at her. "You ready?"

"As I'll ever be."

"Why'd you get me a separate room?" Elena asked, looking around the suite I booked for her that was directly across from mine. "Don't get me wrong this is nice, but I thought…"

"You thought what?" I wanted her to say it. That she thought this weekend meant more than just hanging out like we do back in New York.

Because it does.

When she began to shake her head and walk away, I went after her. I grabbed her by the waist and pulled her close to me.

"Hey… I just figured that you might want your own space." Her back was to me, but she tilted her head back into my chest to look up at me.

"But we always stay together."

"Yea, in New York, Na. We've never been anywhere else together, and I didn't want to assume that you'd want to share a room with me."

She nodded and turned her body to face mine.

"I want to," she whispered. "I came here to spend time with you, and being in separate rooms will cut into that time." I nodded and broke our embrace. Without another word, I gathered her things and made my way across the hall to my room. Once inside, I placed her things in the bedroom and then picked up the phone to call the reception desk to cancel the second room. Just as I was hanging up, Elena came sauntering into the bedroom.

"This suite is amazing," she cooed. "It suits you." I looked her over and smiled at how comfortable she had gotten. The bun that was holding her massive curls was gone, and I had to admit I appreciated the mess that was her hair.

"Yea?"

"Mmhm. It's modern like your apartment, and it screams money, but it's laid back too."

"Like me?"

"Just like you." She laughed and sat on the bed. "I'm hungry. Can we order in, though? I'm kind of tired. I ended up working last night because they were short staffed, but that also means I have an extra day here." I picked up the few menus I had on the dresser and handed them to her.

"So, I have you until Wednesday?"

"Yea, I hope that's cool," she said, scanning over the

menu for one of the hotel restaurants. "I probably should have asked, I know you have a lot of work to do."

I walked into the bathroom while she continued to ramble on about me working and her finding things to do so I don't get behind. I let her talk while running her a bath, and when I was finished, I leaned against the bathroom door frame and watched her.

"I think I want to eat from this place… Blue Hound Kitchen and Cocktails. They have an Ahi Bowl that sounds good, and I've been craving sushi for a few days. Do you think they'll deliver drinks up here too?" I didn't answer her. I just continued to stare.

She was beautiful.

The thought always crosses my mind when she's in my presence.

"Noah?"

"Yea?"

"Did you hear my question?"

"Yea, they'll deliver drinks," I said, answering her question. She stared at me, curiously. Tilting her head sideways as if the move would give her a better read on me. "Come here." She didn't argue or waste any time coming to me. I wrapped one arm around her waist but kept a slight gap between us. "I ran you a bath. Relax, and I'll order the food." She blinked a few times and then shook her head.

"You ran me a bath?" I nodded. It was something I hadn't done before, so the confusion in her tone didn't surprise me. "OK. That was nice of you." She stared up at me, trying to get another read on me, but I quickly kissed her forehead and then pushed her into the bathroom.

"Relax, and I'll come grab you when the food is here." I pulled the bathroom door closed and then released a deep sigh. This weekend would make or break us. I felt that to be true, and it scared me a little, but again the fears didn't trump me wanting to try. If anything, it fueled me to move forward. Shaking away my thoughts, I picked up the menu for Blue Hound kitchen, picked out a few other options to go along with her Ahi Bowl, and then ordered for us. I also ordered two bottles of wine. It was still early in the day, but I had a feeling that we were in for the night, and I was alright with that. More than alright.

HE WANTED US TO STAY IN SEPARATE ROOMS, BUT HE'S running me baths. Noah had never run me a shower before, and he's always enjoyed taking care of me. It's like the minute we met, he took a liking to me. Once we began to learn about each other, he said, that he wanted me to feel like I was important enough to be taken care of. All because I had taken care of my mother and without regret or complaints.

"When you were taking care of everyone else, who was taking care of you?" he asked.

"Me."

"That doesn't count. Everyone needs someone to count on."

"I have Elijah." He shook his head.

"Yea, but he's your brother."

"And he's all I've had since I was thirteen." I shrugged and looked away.

"Elena, have you ever been in love?"

The question threw me. I didn't understand why he'd asked me that, but he had.

"Once," I replied. "But he left, and I let him."

"You let him?"

"Yea, we were young. Early twenties and he got a job in Chicago after graduation. He asked me to go with him, but I had my mother to take care of, and he knew that I wouldn't leave her. He'd asked because he wanted me to say no, so I gave him what he wanted."

Marcus and I had only been together for a couple of years, and though I loved him, I probably wouldn't have followed him even if my mother wasn't sick. He didn't feel like forever for me, and I guess that meant that I had never really been in love. It was how I knew Noah was it for me because I would follow him to the ends of the earth if he asked.

All he had to do was ask.

A chill ran up my spine, and I sighed. I don't know how long I'd been sitting in this tub, but the water was now cold. I let the water out and then turned the shower on. When I'd come in here, I noticed that all the things I used at home were already here. Noah had actually gone out and bought my favorite soap and bubble bath. It was almost as if he were hoping I'd want to stay with him. The thought brought a smile to my face as I lathered up and then scrubbed my skin. I repeated the steps two more times and then cut the water off after rinsing. There was a towel waiting for me on the bathroom sink and a pair of slippers on the floor in front of it. I dried off, wrapped the towel around me, and then pushed my feet into the soft material. I stepped into the bedroom, and to my surprise, Noah had laid out one of his shirts for me and a pair of my biker shorts that he'd obviously gotten out of my suitcase. My cocoa butter body oil was also lying on the bed, ready for me to use.

I wasted no time moisturizing my skin and getting dressed. Afterward, I went in search of Noah. I found him in the living room area of the suite with his laptop in front of him and a deep frown on his face.

"Getting some work done?" I asked, gaining his attention. He shut his laptop, set it aside, and then patted the spot next to him. "You didn't have to stop, I could have—"

"Come sit, Na." I moved toward him and then plopped down in the spot he'd beckoned me to. "How was your bath?"

"Good," I said. "Great. Thank you for getting my favorite things so I could have them."

"Always," he responded, looking me over. "I like you in my shirts."

"I like wearing them." *Especially when they smell like you.* "How long was I in there?"

"An hour. The food should be here soon." As if on cue, there was a knock at the door, and Noah stood to answer. I watched him as he swaggered toward the door in his normal cool like manner. He was always cool, always laid back, always sure of himself, but lately, there's been a shift. I think I'm that shift. The man from the hotel pushed the cart of food in and set it up on the table and then retreated after Noah handed him a tip.

"What else did you order?" I asked, standing to meet him. "That doesn't look like lunch for two." He shrugged and walked into the small kitchenette and grabbed two glasses.

"I wanted variety," he said, taking a bottle of wine from the ice bucket. "Do you want wine now or later."

"Now."

"Now, it is." He poured two hefty glasses and then lifted the tops off the meals. My mouth watered at the sight of everything on display. Along with my Ahi Bowl, he'd ordered fish tacos, street fries—that consisted of French onion dip, cotija cheese, rosemary, and chili—and then there were lamb chops which I was positive were for him. He also ordered two slices of carrot cake. "You're drooling."

"I am not!" I screeched, rubbing my mouth.

"Seemed that way to me," he said, laughing. "Here." He handed me my Ahi Bowl and one of the glasses of wine he'd poured. "Go sit over there." I did as he said and took a seat on the couch. After taking a long sip of the sweet red wine, I dug into my bowl. Noah had a lamb chop in between his lips as he sat down. He cut his eye at me and then bit into it.

"Is that good?" he asked, pointing at my bowl. I hummed in response and then held it out to him.

"You can have some, but I want one of those chops." He smirked and handed the plate over. I knew what he was doing, but I didn't care. I didn't eat much on my own, but when I was with Noah, he somehow always gets me to eat three meals sometimes more. I bit into one of the lamb chops and moaned. The flavor was something else.

"OK. That is good," I complimented, handing him the plate back. I took another sip of my wine while watching him devour the rest of his food. By the time he was finished, I was draining my glass and searching for more. "Do you want more wine?" He looked at his drink, which was still pretty full and shook his head.

"Help yourself, though." *Don't mind if I do.*

I poured another glass and then settled next to him on the couch. He draped an arm around me and pulled me closer to his body.

"So, how did the art gala go the other night?"

"Better than I thought it would," he said. "I found some pieces that have the potential to sell well." I nodded and took another sip of my wine. I was a lightweight and already feeling the effects of it. I unintentionally pressed my nose into Noah's chest and sniffed. I hadn't realized that I'd done it until I felt his body vibrating with laughter.

"Why, when you get drunk, do you sniff me?" He continued to laugh at my expense, but I shrugged off the embarrassment with a laugh of my own.

"I'm not drunk," I argued. I moved away from him, and he laughed harder. "I'm not!"

"Sure, Na, whatever you say."

"I love it when you call me that," I whispered. My statement ceased all laughter from him. The seriousness in his gaze pinned me to my seat. I felt like if I moved, I would be exposing myself to him.

"Tell me something," he started. "The doctor at the hospital that's been asking you out, why have you really been turning him down?"

"Does there have to be an exact reason?" I stood to get away from the suffocating air that was surrounding us. As I poured another glass of wine, I thought about his question. He was the reason, and I had this feeling that he was only asking because he wanted to hear that. Did that mean he wanted us to be something, or was it an ego thing? I debunked that thought seconds later. Noah wasn't a man that wanted or needed his ego stroked.

"There doesn't have to be one, but in this instance, I feel like there is." I sat the bottle down and picked up my glass. I took two big gulps and then turned to face him. "Is there?"

"I—Noah, I'm not sure how you want me to answer that." I shook my head. "No, I'm not sure if you want to hear the answer to that."

"Why are you standing all the way over there?" I waved my hand back and forth between us.

"Because I need space away from you," I said. "It's hot,

and I'm feeling things, and you're acting weird." He chuckled and dropped his head but only for a second.

"You're the one acting weird, Na. I only asked you a simple question."

"You and I both know that question isn't just simple."

"We do?"

"Noah," I groaned. "Why are you doing this right now?" He was acting weird, and it was freaking me out. I now wished I hadn't drunk any wine at all. Maybe I would be handling this situation better. Maybe I am the one that's acting weird. I dropped my shoulders and took deep breaths.

"I just want to know why you won't give him a chance."

"Because nothing about him appeals to me. He doesn't do *it* for me. I don't find him interesting. He's pushy in the worst kind of way, and he's not my type." *You are. It's you!*

"I see," he murmured nodding. "Come here." I shook my head.

"No, I think I like it better over here by the second bottle of wine."

He laughed.

The man was amused, and I didn't find any of this amusing. Does he not know how much I want to blurt out that I love him. That he's the man, I want to date and be with. That I would have his babies, and if they were twins, I would be stoked. He has to know I feel that way. There's no way that the man who seems to know me better than I know myself doesn't know that I'm just that into him.

"Fine, I'll come to you." He stalked toward me, seeming taller than usual, and I backed away. I sucked in a breath when my back hit the hotel room door. "Why are you running from me?"

"Why are you playing with my emotions?" I quipped,

finding some courage. He peered down at me. Those deep brown pools of his had me feeling as if I were drowning. My body was enjoying the adrenalin rush. My vagina wanted him to speak to her. *Oh God. I'm losing it.*

"That isn't my intention."

"Noah, you can't do this to me right now."

"Do what?" he asked. I knew he genuinely wanted to know. The curiosity in his tone and the question deep in his gaze told me so. "Tell me what I'm doing to you, Na. And then tell me if you want me to stop."

"I-I want you," I said, throwing myself off. "I mean, I… *fuck.* I don't know."

"You want me?" I nodded. Once again, throwing myself off. At this point, my mind was speaking for me, and I had no control over what was happening. I was answering questions he hadn't even asked. This was turning into a disaster. "What if I said that I wanted you too, how would that make you feel?" His body felt closer. I was gazing up into his eyes, not breaking contact, even though I wanted to. I wanted to slip away and run, but I also wanted to face what was happening. Is this why he asked me here? "Na."

"I-It would make me happy," I answered truthfully. "I want you to want me."

"Yea?" I nodded and looked away.

He grabbed my chin and turned my head back to him. With his eyes on me again, he smiled and then did the last thing I ever expected him to do. He kissed me. It was soft, sweet, and quick. As fast as our lips had met was as quickly as they were separated, but I felt every bit of it. I felt every bit of *him.*

"I want you," he confessed, stepping away from me. "And for some reason, my sister and your brother, along with the rest of our friends, seem to think that if we don't try, we'll lose each other, and I can't have that, Na." He shook his head as if thinking about losing me was hurting him. "I can't lose you no matter how scared I am of trying this love thing again."

"You're scared?"

"You have no idea how scared I am." I stepped toward him and reached for his hand. "The fact that I even feel comfortable enough telling you that scares the fuck out of me, but losing you scares me more."

"I—you won't lose me."

"How can you be sure?" he asked, staring at me. "How can you be sure that if this doesn't work that we won't drift apart?"

"I guess I'm not sure, but Noah, I'm scared too. I'm scared that if we don't explore what's so obvious between us that we'll resent each other. I've been trying to be just your friend since the beginning. You've intrigued me since that first meeting, and I haven't been able to get enough of you. I can't date that doctor or anyone else for that matter because they aren't you."

The next thing I knew, his lips were crashing into mine, and everything else around us became a blur. This was happening.

8

Noah

FUCK.

THIS WAS HAPPENING.

I stared down at Elena's naked body and tried to recount our steps. How did we get here so fast, and damn was she beautiful. The clothes she wear does her body no justice.

"You're beautiful," I said, leaning forward to capture her lips once again. "Fucking stunning."

"Sounds different when you're saying it while I'm completely exposed to you."

"And I'm speaking all facts," I countered, pressing my lips into her neck and then trailing down to her breasts. "I would never lie to you," I added, before taking her nipple into my mouth and sucking. I've dreamt about having her like this. She had me feeling like a teenager these last few months. Wanting her so bad that I looked forward to sleeping so I could pretend like she was mine. Her moans sounded better than in my dreams, though. Her skin was softer too, and she smelled like heaven—whatever that smelled like.

"Noah," she breathed. I ignored the plea and

continued to take my time with her. I needed time to explore. To get acclimated with her body. With my eyes trained on hers, I placed light kisses down her toned stomach until I was face to face with her waxed mound. It was a fresh wax too. I licked my lips and used my thumb to part her lips, giving me a view of her wet center.

"Beautiful," I mumbled, going in for a quick taste. "Mmm."

"N-Noah… what are… what are we doing?"

"We are doing exactly what we've been avoiding," I said, before running the tip of my tongue over her clit a few times. "What we are both scared of but have no need to be." We could work through all of the bullshit together. Communication was key, and Elena and I did that well.

She lifted her pelvis, and I took that as her finally giving in to me. I dove in face first and didn't pull back. She tasted fucking amazing, and the way she was grinding her clit into my tongue told me all I needed to know. My baby was nasty, and she wanted everything I wanted to give her.

"Oh God," she cried, trying to move away. I gripped her waist and pulled her back. I dipped my tongue into her wet tunnel and then dragged it back her clit and sucked faster. She was close. And fuck me if her moans didn't have me ready to bust prematurely. They sounded like pure music to my ears. "I-I'm going to…" She never finished that statement. Her body seized in my arms, and I continued to eat until she came down from her high. A deep sigh filled the room, and then giggles followed. I stared at Elena in awe and then chuckled.

"You're drunk," I said, lifting my body and leaning it over hers.

"I'm not drunk… I'm just shocked."

"And you giggle when you're shocked." It wasn't a

question. She smiled and then looked away from me. "Let me see your eyes, Na." She slowly brought them back to me as I positioned myself at her opening. "Can I have you?"

"Y-yes." I nodded and grabbed the condom I placed under the pillow when we first pushed our way into the bedroom. I ripped the gold package open and pulled the lubricated rubber from it. With my eyes on Elena, I rolled it on and secured it at the base of my penis. I then leaned for, tilted her head back, and then kissed her lips. I would never get enough of having her like that. Like this. Vulnerable and open to me.

"I swear I'll be good to you," I whispered in her ear and then pushed my way inside of her. I had to pause before moving. She was tight and gripping the fuck out of me.

"Please," she begged. "I need you." I pulled out of her and then dipped back in slowly, repeating the move over and over until she was begging me to give her more. To fuck her harder.

"Na, this shit is deadly, baby girl," I confessed, digging deeper. I dipped in and out of her, bringing the tip of my dick to her opening and then surging forward with the deep strokes she was begging for.

"Yes," she moaned, scraping her fingernails over my back. "God. You're good. So good." She wrapped her legs around my waist and began to meet my every stroke. "Noah… I-I—"

"I need you to cum for me, baby," I growled. "I won't last too much longer." I closed my eyes and buried myself deeper. Giving her everything I had. My body was begging for a release, and she was pulling it out of me. *Fuck.* "Na —" Her pussy clamped around me, and her soft moans of pleasure cut me off. She was giving me what I asked for, and it was better than I thought it would be. Her pleasure stricken face was a beautiful sight to see, and soon after she began to shake beneath me, I released into the condom. "Fuck." I fell forward but balanced myself as best I could on my forearms.

"That was—"

"Amazing," I finished for her. After a few minutes, I slowly pulled myself from inside of her and climbed out of bed to get rid of the condom. I made quick of the job and was back to her in a matter of seconds. I wasted no time securing her body close to mine.

"If this was supposed to set the tone for this weekend, then I'm all for how it went," she said, kissing my chest.

"I have to agree with you." Silence followed, and I knew both of our minds were still reeling from what we just did but also trying to figure out what it all meant. I hadn't expected things to go like this. I didn't ask her to come here for sex. I just wanted to spend time with her away from everyone else, in a city where no one knew who we were. I wanted to see if she felt for me what I thought she did. And damn if she didn't prove that and then some. I guess the question now is, where do we go from here? "You good?"

"I'm great," she muttered. "I—Noah, things won't change between us, will they?"

"They might, but maybe for the better."

"And if we fuck this up?" That was my fear.

"Then we figure out how to fix it, baby." I kissed her forehead and pulled her closer. "I care about you a lot. I have from the moment we met, and I want this thing to happen. I want us to try, but we both have to understand that shit may never be the same. The consequences could be detrimental, but the reward... the reward could be life changing."

"I want the life changing part." She sighed and then added. "Noah, I'm scared."

"Me too, Na," I admitted, for the millionth time tonight. "Me too." We didn't have shit figured out, but that's life, right?

There was so much we needed to talk about, but it didn't need to be the focal point of this weekend. I wouldn't let it.

"Let's just focus on enjoying each other this weekend, and we'll figure out the rest when we get back to New York, alright?" The response I got was soft snores.

Laughing, I shifted my body some and then quietly slipped out of bed. I pulled the blanket over her naked body, tossed on a pair of basketball shorts, and then left the room after one last look. I grabbed my laptop, phone, and headed out onto the balcony. I checked and replied to a few emails before checking my phone. There were a few missed business calls that didn't need attention right away and a missed call from Semaj. We didn't talk often, but something was telling me that I knew exactly what this call was about.

"Noah, fucking White," he boomed. "You're a genius. Have you ever thought about becoming an agent."

"Not even once," I said, laughing. "I take it my advice brought about some good results."

"Something like that, and I want to thank you."

"No need to thank me, man," I said, brushing it off. I didn't do anything special. "I'm just glad things are working out. Speaking of, how's therapy?"

"It's a bunch of bullshit, but don't tell my doctor you heard me complaining she's been on my ass." I heard a voice in the background that was muffled, and then it became clear.

"I know you aren't sitting in my office talking about

me, Semaj," the soft voice called out. She was definitely a southern belle. Her accent was thick and hard to miss. "Keep at it, and I'm going to hurt your other leg."

"I think you just want to keep me around longer," he replied. I could hear the amusement in his tone. "Aye, Noah, I have to go, but thanks again." The line went dead, and I shook my head. Semaj and Samir were brothers, but two totally different people, and it was funny seeing the differences up close. When I had decided that I could catch some sleep with Elena, my phone rang.

"This is Noah."

"Mr. White, this is Tim Reed from Harpers Art Gallery."

"Mr. Reed, I take it you heard back from Jameson." I could hear shuffling in the background, and then his voice cut into the noise.

"Yes, he wanted to know if you could meet tomorrow afternoon here at the gallery."

I immediately wanted to say no, and it was on the tip of my tongue to do so, but then I changed my mind. This deal could be lucrative, and I didn't want to miss out on it, so I agreed to meet with him. I knew Elena would understand if I needed to handle business for a couple of hours while she chilled out here by the pool or something.

"Ok great, tomorrow at two o'clock. I'll let him know, and I'll see you then." After ending the call, I set aside my laptop and phone and walked over to the balcony to get a better look at what was happening down below. The side of the hotel I was on gave me the perfect view of downtown Phoenix. It was nothing like seeing the busy streets of New York, but I liked being able to see people in their element. It was a form of therapy for me. I wonder if Elena missed being in a slower moving city. I sometimes wonder if New York isn't for me anymore. I enjoy having access to my family and friends when I need them, but it doesn't feel like home anymore. And when I visit places like Arizona or Texas where it's slower and always warmer, I get ideas of raising a family here. I can remember talking to Corrie about it and her waving the idea off. She was all about New York and places like it. It didn't surprise me that she ended up in a place that had a high tourist rate like back home. The more I think about our relationship, the more I began to see how different we were.

"I love New York, but I miss this," Elena said, stepping closer to me. "I mean Detroit is a pretty busy city but nothing like New York." I looked over at her, and she looked content. Happy. "What are you doing out here?"

"I was getting some work done while you slept." I threw an arm over her shoulder and pulled her closer. "Did you get enough sleep?" She shook her head.

"No, but you were gone when I reached for you, and it woke me." She snuggled closer to me and sighed. "I like that you know how I feel now."

"Do I know exactly how you feel?" I had a feeling she was holding back and rightfully so.

"I guess not, but you know enough, and I'm glad that you do."

"Yea, me too."

"I think we'll be OK, what about you?"

"I'm thinking the same thing." It was too soon to tell, but I appreciated the confidence she had in us, and I welcomed it.

9

Elena

"HEY, DAD." I WAS SITTING OUT ON THE BALCONY READING the book I brought along for my plane ride when his call came through. I thought about not answering again, but what was the point. I loved my father, and though I thought he was a selfish man, I still needed him. And if that meant only phone calls, then I would deal with that.

"I take it this means you aren't mad anymore.

"Wrong," I quipped. "I'm still upset, but I'll get over it."

"Elena, prison is no place for my daughter."

"And if we're being technical, then a prison is no place for my father." I said the words before I could stop myself, and his silence told me everything I needed to know. I had outed myself. "Dad—"

"You know?"

"I've known for a long time." It was true. My mom would ramble about how she never meant for him to take on her wrong doings, and at first, I was confused by it, but then I began to put the pieces together. After realizing what she was saying, I asked my aunt, and against her better judgment, she told me everything. And when Elijah had given up on helping our dad's case, I realized that he knew too. That would be the only thing that would stop him from pursuing it further. "Look. I know that you feel like you're protecting me, but I don't need protecting from you. I've been good for a long time, and you being in prison didn't help me get there. What I need from you is the time that I don't get. The time that I've missed out on all these years. So if your only excuse is that a prison isn't a place for your daughter, then I call bullshit. Maybe Elijah is right. Maybe you will never see things our way, and I should let the idea go."

"Maybe I should give you both what you want," he said sighing. "All of this time, I've been trying to protect both of you from my bullshit, and I see it's only made you resent me."

"I don't resent you... I just need you. We need you." There was a brief silence, and then he sighed again.

"I'll add you to my visitation list," he finally said. "Bring your brother if he's up for it, and I'll explain everything." The automated system cut in, letting us know that the call would end soon, and I wanted to cry. For the first time in a long time, I felt like we had finally gotten somewhere.

"Thanks, dad."

"Don't thank me just yet, baby girl," he said. "I love you."

"I love you too." The call ended, and I wiped away my tears.

"This is stupid," I mumbled, standing and reentering the suite. I was sitting cooped up in the room, waiting for Noah to get back from his meeting when I could be down by the pool, enjoying the weather that we don't have in New York right now. The heat here was ridiculous but perfect for a quick dip. I grabbed my red two-piece and slipped it onto my body. I placed my sunglasses on my face, stuck my feet into my sandals, picked up my phone, and headed for the pool. I remembered Noah saying that they had one on the rooftop, so I went there. I stepped out onto the roof and smiled at how beautiful it was. I was serious when I said this place suited Noah. It felt like we were chilling at his luxury apartment instead of a hotel. There was a section of couches that were calling my name, but I went for the pool instead. I stepped out of my sandals and sat at the edge of the pool, dipping my feet into the cool water. After I was comfortable, I opened the group text thread I had with the ladies and sent one off.

Me: *So…*

Juniper: *You got some dick?*

She was joking but had no idea how right she was. I didn't want to disclose that just yet.

Magnolia: *Have some manners, Juni. But seriously, did you get some dick?"*

Nova: *Please, guys, because I'm scared to hear the answer to this question. She's in Arizona with Noah.*

I laughed, envisioning the grimace on her face.

Lilac: *wait…*

Lilac*: In Arizona with Noah?*

Blossom: *So does that mean you guys are a thing now?*

Brynlee: *Can we let her tell us what's happening before we assume.*

Daisy: *Present… You may now reply.*

She knew exactly what I was waiting for. I needed all of the replies to come through before I responded because if I gave up anything while someone was missing, I would have to repeat myself later.

Me: *I think Noah and I are exploring something more. The friendship has officially advanced, and I'm freaking terrified.*

Brynlee: *Aww babe, but this is what you want, right?*

Me: *Yes, but what if things go wrong and I lose him as my friend.*

Nova: *Fear will only hold you back. As long as you guys are honest with each other about what you want, then things will go as they should.*

Magnolia: *To play off what Nova said, I believe that it's okay to be afraid, but don't let that sway your decisions. Think things through and communicate with him. It'll all work out. You guys are obviously meant to be.*

Juniper: *I agree with the ladies, now did you finally get some dick?*

Nova: *Please spare me…*

I didn't spare her at all. It was payback for the times she bragged about my brother. For the next hour, I chilled by the pool, texting back and forth with the ladies and scrolling on social media. I was about to call it a day and head back to the room to wait for Noah, but a dark figure stood over me, and when I tilted my head back to find him standing there, my heart flipped in my chest. He was shirtless, in his swim trunks and a towel was draped around his neck.

"Wassup, beautiful," he spoke, sitting next to me. I took off my sunglasses and set them next to my sandals.

"Hey, you," I whispered, bumping shoulders with him. "Did your meeting go good?"

"Yea, I spent some money and then made some money, so it was productive." Before I could respond, he dropped his body into the water, and when he surfaced, he had this mischievous look on his face.

"Don't you dare, Noah." He ignored me and pulled my body right in with him. The cold water hit me, and I felt like I would freeze to death. "I am going to kill you."

"Who comes to the pool to sit and play on their

phone?" he asked, pulling my body to him and backing me into a corner.

"How do you know I didn't get in before you got here?"

"Because your hair is too dry, Na." He pulled it out of the loose bun and ran his fingers through my curls. At least he managed to get them through the kinks. "I like it better when you wear it down." He then scooped up some water and dumped it over my head to wet my hair.

"Hey! The chlorine will mess with my curls."

"I'm sure they won't suffer too bad." He pressed his forehead into mine and kissed my lips. "I missed you."

"More than usual?"

"Yea. It's like yesterday sparked something inside of me. I always miss you when we're apart, but today was different." I wrapped my arms around his waist and pressed my chin into his chest.

"How so?"

"I kept wondering if you came up here to relax or if you were reading a book in the room with a glass of wine. Then I thought, Nah, she's gossiping on the phone with the girls. I went back and forth with those, and then I figured you'd done them all. I couldn't wait to find out if I was right. I was anticipating seeing your face so I could kiss you. I—it was just a lot of shit that I don't normally allow myself to think about."

"So, did I do them all?" He gave me a questioning look, but it disappeared just as quickly as it had appeared.

"Yea, you did," he answered. "I saw the book on the balcony and the empty glass sitting next to it. And obviously, you were up here by the pool since this is where I found you."

"And about me gossiping to the girls?" He smirked.

"Nova called me." I groaned and playfully rolled my eyes.

"Your sister is a snitch."

"It's a twin thing," he defended. "She tries to keeps secrets, and then she doesn't try. I'm the same with her, though." He leaned forward and kissed me again. It was already becoming normal for us. It was easy with no thought put into it, and I liked that. I liked that this was easy for him. At least the kissing part was easy. "I'm hungry."

"Me too. I think I've been out in the sun long enough."

"Good," he said. "I made us reservations for later, but we can grab lunch at the grill up here. I nodded and let him lead me out of the pool. He used the towel that he'd brought for himself and dried me off. "Anyone ever told you that red is your color?"

"As a matter fact they have," I replied, smiling. He was the first to ever tell me that. The night that we met, I wore a red dress, and the first thing he'd said to me was that's your color. "I've added more reds to my wardrobe because of it."

"Yea?" I nodded and slipped my fingers through his outstretched hand. "I'm glad I could influence this."

"I'm sure you are." He laughed and guided us to the grill that was on the rooftop. This felt light and freeing being up here with here and having no worries. I knew it wouldn't last forever, but I wanted to enjoy it while we had the opportunity.

I WALKED into the steamy bathroom naked and slid the shower door open. Noah glanced over his shoulder but didn't acknowledge my intrusion. His muscular body was standing directly under the waterfall shower head.

"Are you coming in, or are you going to watch me from out there?" he asked, turning to face me. I stepped inside with my eyes on his growing erection. "You like what you see?"

"I do actually," I answered. "It's a work of art. Goes perfect with your field of work." He threw his head back and barked out a deep rumble of laughter.

"I like the sound of that."

"I bet you do." I held up the shampoo bottle I'd brought in with me. "I was going to ask if you'd lather me up since it's your fault that it got wet, but I think I have a better idea now."

"We might be able to work something else out." He walked toward me and took the bottle of shampoo from my hands. He then slipped behind me and pushed me toward the waterfall. "Wet your hair for me." I did as he asked. I have low porosity hair, so it took a hot second to get it completely wet, but when I finished, I tried to turn around, but he stopped me. He pulled me into his body and pressed his lips to my ear. "Bend over and press your hands to the wall."

Excitement began to bubble in my stomach as I did what he asked.

"Don't turn around." I nodded and bit down on my lip. The sound of the shampoo bottle being opened, and then him squeezing some out filled the space around us. He placed the bottle in the opening above my head and then dropped his hands into my hair. My mouth fell open as he slipped his dick inside of me at the same time. I was completely outdone. He had the nerve to be massaging my scalp and pussy at the same time.

"Ooh," I moaned, throwing my ass back to meet his strokes. "That feels so good, baby."

"Which part," he asked. "My hands or my dick?"

"B-both." I wanted to turn my head so I could see his face, but I didn't. "Please don't stop."

"I don't plan on it until this pussy is coming, and your scalp is squeaky clean."

Who was this man?

10

Noah

No, seriously, don't laugh," Elena said, smiling. "Elijah was the worst before things went to shit. We had so much fun playing tricks on each other, though. It's a shame we had to grow up so fast." The light in her eyes dimmed a little, but it didn't stop her from smiling. "We had a good life at one point."

"How was it after your pop was gone?"

"Horrible." She sipped on her drink and huffed. "It's like everything that we were shielded from came to light. My dad was really the rock we didn't even know we had. My mom was on drugs heavy back then, and my aunt took care of us until she was out of rehab. And when she did come home, she tried her best, but she was lacking a little. At the time, I didn't understand why she seemed so depressed, but after she got sick, and I learned the truth, it became clear. She was free but not really. The guilt of what she'd done ate at her, and I truly believe that's what made her sick. It's like she wanted to forget, and God gave her what she wanted."

"The more you share with me, the more I see how

strong you are, Na," I said, leaning back in my seat. We were eating at Bobby-Q BBQ Restaurant and Steakhouse. When I'd met up with Jameson earlier today, he gave me the recommendation.

"I'm not that strong." I shook my head.

"Yea, you are, and don't ever doubt it again." She smiled at me and shook her head. Probably thinking about how bossy she thinks I am.

"He's letting me see him finally," she said, watching me through a hooded gaze. "I think me ignoring him worked, but then again, there's something he's been hiding."

"What makes you think that?"

"It's the only thing that makes sense, you know?" I nodded. Her pop's actions were a little weird to me, but I just thought he wanted to protect her. I wouldn't want my daughter visiting me behind bars, but if it's the only way I would get to see her, then I would do it. "Elijah must think the same thing."

"Well, you know I got you if you need me."

"I know. You always do."

"Always will."

"I wish I could say I don't believe you, but I do," she said, biting down on her lip. "It's weird, but I trust you."

"That's weird, why?"

"I trust you completely, Noah," she clarified. "Not just a little bit or only in some areas. No, I trust you without any conditions." *Damn.*

I was honored to have that type of trust from her. It moved me to make sure I never fucked it up. That should feel like a lot of pressure, but it didn't. Maybe because I trusted her just the same.

"I trust you too," I admitted. "Without any conditions and all that good shit."

"Yea?" I nodded.

"But I have to admit that I feel like I'm going to fuck this up with you." She tilted her head at me, and I explained further. "I've only been in one serious relationship, Na. I don't know how to be with anyone else, and somehow I fucked up with the one person I was supposed to know how to be with."

"That's what you think?" she asked. "That you fucked up, and that's why she left." I shrugged. It was how I felt, and because of that, I didn't feel like I deserved to have Elena. She was too good for me, but the thought of her being with someone else did something to my heart. I couldn't have that, so instead of pushing her away, I'm trying. Instead of losing her forever, I'm being open and honest. It helped that she made that part easy for me. It was weird, but what I had with Corrie took fourteen years, but I have that, and then some with Elena and we are just coming up on a year. "She lost out on you, Noah. It's not the other way around. You didn't fuck up, she did. I would be surprised if she didn't try to come back."

"I used to think that's what would happen," I said. "I think that's why in the beginning I was alright. It hadn't fully hit me."

"Do you still want that?" Her eyes were searching mine for the answer before I could even speak. "Because if so I—"

"Don't finish that." I reached across the table and grabbed her hand. "If I still had hope for Corrie and me, you and I wouldn't be a thing, Na. I think you know me better than that to think that I would ever play with your emotions like that. You trust me, right?"

"Yes," she answered, without hesitation.

"Good, because I'll never lie to you," I reminded her. "Even if it'll hurt you." She nodded and reached for the last piece of brisket from the platter we had during dinner. We'd been done eating for at least two hours. The night was going too good, and ending it just to end up back in our room didn't seem right.

"You know," she started, mouth full of food. "I keep wondering how things will be once we are both back in New York."

"I guess we'll see once we are back, won't we?" Though I didn't say it, I was wondering the same thing.

A few hours later, we were back in the suite and out on the balcony.

"Downtown looks so much better at night," Elena said from her spot by the railing. I was sitting in the seat behind her with my eyes on her ass. She had on one of my shirts, and it was slowly riding up, giving me a nice view of the lacy thong she was wearing. "I love this place. The heat is ridiculous, but I still love it."

"Do you see yourself living in New York forever?"

"Hell no," she blurted, turning to give me the perfect view of her beautiful face. "I mean… it's great there, but I could never see myself raising a family there."

"Where at then?" I picked up my phone and snapped a picture of her. "Detroit?"

"Not there either too many bad memories." I snapped another pic and then handed her my phone.

"You're good at this."

"So, where then?" I asked, getting the conversation back on track. She shrugged.

"I don't know. I like it here." She handed my phone back to me and then posted back up on the railing. "I think being down south would be nice. I like Georgia, and Texas is nice too. South Carolina is a little too slow, but North Carolina has a nice city feel in some places."

"You would leave your mom and brother?"

"I've lived away from Elijah before, so that part would be easy, but leaving my mom would be hard. The idea of uprooting her again isn't appealing either. She has the best care where she currently is." She walked toward me and then climbed into my lap. "Sometimes I think that I'll be stuck because I don't want to be away from her. I feel guilty for wanting to have a life."

"You shouldn't."

"I know, but it's hard not to." I wrapped my arms around her waist and kissed her lips. "I know it's crazy but—"

"It's not crazy," I said. "I understand, and I admire how selfless you are. It's one of the things I love about you. Just know that it's OK to be selfish sometimes too."

"I'm being selfish right now," she murmured into my ear. "You're the best part of this weekend full of selfish acts."

"I'm glad I can be the best part of anything that has to do with you." I smacked her ass, and she yelped. "Quit grinding that hot ass pussy on me, girl."

"But I want you," she groaned. She proceeded to pull at my shorts until my dick was out. I hooked my finger into her thong and pulled it to the side.

"Have me then, Na." I smacked her ass again, and she lifted up. "Show me what you got." She lowered herself onto me with her eyes trained on mine. The exchange was simple but intense, and when she began to move, I was done for.

"I'll never get enough of this."

"You don't have to." I was going to make sure of that.

ME: *How's my niece or nephew?*

Nova: *I don't know. Doing what babies do. Cook.*

Me: *You're weird, you know that?*

Nova: *We're twins, did you forget?*

I glanced over at a sleeping Elena and smirked. Closing out of my text thread with Nova, I opened the camera and snapped a few pictures of her. I sent them to her and then went back to reply to Nova's message.

Me: *I need a favor.*

Nova: *Depends on how time consuming it is.*

I sent her the picture I'd taken of Elena out on the balcony a few hours ago with a message attached that said, *Can you bring that to life.*

Nova: *Wow. Did you take that of her? She's fucking gorgeous.*

Me: *Yea, this iPhone eleven camera makes me feel like a pro, and I keep telling her that it needs to be a portrait, but she just waved me off. So, can you hook it up?*

Nova: *I got you.*

Me: *Have I ever told you that you're my favorite sister?*

Nova: *Bye! I'm your only sister.*

"Are you texting a girl I don't know about," Elena grumbled. I looked at her, and she had one eye trained on me. "Because I swear I'll have her jumped."

"What makes you think I'm texting a girl?" I set my phone down between us, and she glanced at it.

"Because you looked happy. I don't know."

Laughing, I said, "Talking to my sister usually makes me happy. It's a—"

"Twin thing," she finished. "I know." She yawned and closed her eyes. "Talking to you makes me happy."

She was asleep again before I could tell her that the feeling was mutual. I watched her sleep until my own eyes began to get heavy. I slid my phone under the pillow and then pulled her body close to mine. She groaned the whole time, but the second our skin made contact, she sighed and snuggled closer. I kissed her forehead and fell into a deep sleep shortly after that.

"HELLO, WELCOME TO OTIS," THE HOSTESS GREETED. I smiled and nodded while looking around for Elijah. I spotted him sitting in the back and made my way to him. As I approached, I took note of the annoyed look on his face. His phone was gripped tightly in his hand as he stared down at the screen. His tense demeanor unnerved me.

"Lijah, are you OK?" I asked. He looked up from his phone and then stood. After he kissed my cheek, we both took our seats. "Why do you look like you want to set this place on fire?"

"This case I'm working is taking a turn for the worse, but I'll worry about that after we eat." He stuffed his phone into his pocket and gave me his undivided attention. The waitress came over and took our orders. The second she was gone, Elijah jumped right into his questioning. "How was Arizona?"

I smiled.

"I feel like you know the answer to that already." He shook his head.

"I don't," he said. "Nova is actually keeping secrets

well. I could have probably gotten it out of her, but I didn't want to give up a lung for it." I laughed. Nova was weird like that. If you wanted information out of her, you had to give her something in return. Money or something material wouldn't work. Noah owes her a kidney and a slew of other things.

"I mean, things went well. I think we figured out what we want from each other, but it'll take time to actually get there." He nodded.

"No need to rush," he suggested. "Let things play out." And that was the end of that. Elijah wasn't one to delve too deep into my business. Recently was the most he'd been interested in my love life. As long as the man treated me right then, he was good, but obviously, things were a little different.

I took a couple sips of my sprite and prepared myself for where this conversation was going. We didn't meet to talk about my situation with Noah. That was far left from what this was really about.

"So… about dad," I muttered.

"How long have you known?" he asked, leaning back in his seat.

"A while," I answered. "I found out right after you decided to take on his case." The look on his face was blank. There was nothing there for me to read.

"Why didn't you say anything, Lena?"

"I—honestly, I was trying to keep things how they were. I didn't want to add to what we were already dealing with. We'd been through so much, Lijah, and I was tired of dealing. I was tired of our lives being about what dad did. I also knew that telling you would only discourage you from your job. You only became a lawyer for dad, but I knew you'd be great at it." His lips quirked up a bit, and then he chuckled.

"So, all of this time, you've been taking care of me."

I didn't answer him for a minute because I hadn't thought about it that way. I was good at taking care of people, but it never occurred to me that the roles had switched between Elijah and me.

"I didn't think of it that way."

"I'm supposed to protect you," he said.

"And you did." I pointed between us. "We were each other's rock all those years, but when you went off to college, I had to figure somethings out on my own, and I'm grateful for that. It made me stronger. I knew I had you, but I also knew that if I needed to take care of myself, I could." He sighed and leaned forward.

"That was hard for me." He shook his head. "Leaving you alone. I didn't want to but—"

"But you did what you needed, and things weren't as bad then. Ma was a little bit better until she wasn't."

"I should've come home when she got sick."

"Don't do that," I started. "You took a job in one of the best cities in the world. I would have cussed you out if you had turned it down." I knew he felt bad about leaving me to take care of our mother, but in reality, it was my decision to do it. I wasn't forced, and him being gone didn't force my hand. I did it because I wanted to, and when things had gotten worse, I asked for help. And when I did that, he showed up and did what he needed for me. For *us*.

"What do you want to do about dad?" he asked. "Are we meeting him or…" His voice trailed.

"You would come?"

He furrowed his eyebrows and said, "I would never let you face that alone. Never."

"I want to go."

"Then we're going," he said with finality. Our food

came out, and we ended the intense conversation. It didn't occur to me that I needed to have this talk with him, but I appreciated being able to. It made me feel light.

"When does Noah come back?"

"Next Friday." He barely got any work done while I was there—his choice—and because of that, he decided to stay longer. I had only been back in New York for a day, and I missed him like crazy. I missed him more than usual, and I couldn't wait to see his face again. Up, close, and personal.

"HEY, HANDSOME," I greeted, answering Noah's facetime call. Twenty-four hours away from this man and I couldn't stand it.

He smiled at me and then said, "Wassup, beautiful. How was your day?" I laid on my side and propped my phone up on a pillow.

"It was OK." I slipped my arm under my pillow and pulled it closer. "I would rather be where you are, though."

"I wish you were still here, too, even though I probably wouldn't get any work done."

I rolled my eyes.

"Don't blame me for that." I laughed. "You enjoyed not getting any work done because of me." I bit down on my lip. Thoughts of the things he'd done to my body swarmed around in my mind. Noah was good with his hands, mouth, and all the above. No man had ever made me feel as good as he did.

"It was worth it," he agreed. "More than worth it."

"Yea?"

"Mmhm."

"Elijah and I are going to see my dad this upcoming weekend."

"Are you ready for that?" I shook my head.

"Not really, but I need it to happen."

"I wish I could be there for you."

"Just… be available to take my call after it's over."

He had a thoughtful look on his face as he said, "I can do that for you, baby."

"Call me that again."

"You look beautiful as hell right now, baby," he said, obliging to my request and adding on some extra love for me.

"I look a mess. My hair is—"

"You look beautiful like I said," he countered. "And your hair is exactly how I like it. Wild and untamed."

I couldn't stop myself from smiling. Why did he have to say things like that to me? Didn't he know that it only made me love him more?

"Noah, I can't… I won't be able to not fall for you." *I already have.* "If you aren't sure that—"

"I'm sure, Na," he interjected. "I'm sure that I want you. I want more than what we had." There was nothing but sincerity in his tone and eyes.

"OK." I closed my eyes while smiling. I wanted to stay on the phone with him but… "I need to get some sleep before my shift tonight." I opened my eyes to find him staring at me.

"Get some sleep, baby, and call me on your break."

"It'll be at like four in the morning."

"Has that ever mattered?" I shook my head.

"OK, I'll call you on my break."

It took a minute for me to fall asleep, but when I did, my dreams consisted of Noah's tongue pleasuring me until I orgasmed over and over. When I woke, I was beyond frustrated and even more agitated that it hadn't been real. After shutting the bathroom door, I hung my towel up on the hook behind it and then stepped into the running shower. I let the hot water massage my tight muscles for as long as time would allow. It was going on nine at night, and I had two hours before my shift started. I had gotten all of five hours of sleep, and that wasn't exactly enough, but it would do. I enjoyed the hot water for a little longer and then washed up. After getting out, I took my time moisturizing my body and then dressed in my scrubs. I quickly did my hair, grabbed the lunch I'd made before talking to Noah, and then headed out early.

I still had possession of Nova's truck on most days because Elijah liked to drive her around. While heading to Manhattan, I decided to call Noah. I was missing him and needed to hear his voice before my lunch break.

"You headed in?" he asked after answering.

"Yes, and I wanted to hear your voice again."

"You miss me?" His tone was deep but soft. There was so much feeling in that question.

"I really do. I get what you were saying about it being different."

"I'm glad I'm not the only one experiencing it." I smiled at the thought of him missing me just as much as I missed him. Knowing that the feeling was mutual did something to me.

"I was thinking… when you get back that I can treat you to something."

"Like what?"

"I haven't thought that far yet, but it'll be a date." He deserved to be treated. Noah does too much for me, and I want to show him my appreciation.

"I'm open to it." There was a brief silence, and then he

added, "I'm open to exploring a lot of things with you, Na, but be patient with me. Can you do that?"

"Yea, I can do that," I agreed without hesitation. He wasn't asking for a lot. I knew in my heart that this was a lot for him, and to be honest, it was for me too. Both of our hearts were on the line here, and we needed to be careful.

"Thanks, Na."

"Don't thank me just yet, big guy," I joked. As I pulled into the Presbyterian parking lot, I smiled. "I'm at work so I'll—"

"On your break," he said, cutting in. "I want to hear from you on your break, baby girl."

"You will," I replied, still smiling.

"I love you."

"I... I love you too, Noah."

God, I loved him so much.

I remember when I first came to the conclusion that I loved him more than just a friend. The second it hit me, my body almost gave out on me.

"Have you ever thought about what it would have been like if we'd met years ago?" I asked, digging into the popcorn bowl that sat in between us. "I mean... I know you were with Corrie but—"

"If I would have met you back then..." he paused and glanced at me. The look in his eyes hit me hard. There was so much... passion. So much of something that I couldn't quite read, but I felt. "I don't think Corrie and I would have been a thing."

His words hit me, and it was then that I realized he was mine. Noah belonged to me, and he had even before we met. We may have some things to overcome, but I know the outcome will be worth it. He'll be worth it. I had faith in the bond we share, but more importantly, I have faith in him.

```
┌─────────────────────────────────┐
│                                 │
│              12                 │
│                                 │
│             Noah                │
│                                 │
└─────────────────────────────────┘
```

ELENA: *I NEED YOU.*

She sent that text three hours ago. When I got it, I called her immediately, but there was no answer. I've been calling Elena for the last two hours nonstop, and nothing has come of it. Something was happening because I couldn't get in touch with Nova or Elijah either. She wasn't visiting her father until Sunday, and today was Friday. When I'd talked to her early this morning, she told me she was going to visit her mother and then it hit me. Something had to have happened to her mother. So here I was walking through the Phoenix Sky Harbor International Airport, headed back to New York. Headed back to Elena.

I walked toward my gate with my mind racing. I hadn't gotten as close to as much work done as I needed to, but none of that was important. The only thing that would calm my mind and heart was getting to Elena. She was all that mattered in this moment, and as I reached my designated gate, I realized that I loved her. That I was in love with her, and it didn't matter that I felt unworthy or that my past relationship hadn't worked. She was who I was supposed to be with, and I learned long ago that God has a way of rearranging your life for the better.

Is that what he had done?

Had he removed Corrie from my life to make room for Elena?

Was she my predestined soulmate?

I believed in those at one point. I'd even thought that Corrie was it. We were so young when we met. She was the new kid at school, and I was the popular rich kid that didn't act like one. She cornered me after I had taken up for her one day. I fell in love immediately, but as time passed. Things changed. We changed.

We became adults, and though we were still in love—at least I thought so—it wasn't the same. It took until just now for me to see that God had been giving me signs all this time. He'd been trying to warn me that Corrie wasn't the one. It took fourteen years for me to see it.

It took *her* leaving me for me to see it.

"Why now?" I asked, staring at Corrie's beautiful face. She looked so content in her decision to end this. To end us. And deep down, I didn't feel like fighting.

"Noah, we've been together for so long," she murmured, looking away from me. Her eyes were trained on the city below. The large bay window had always been her favorite. It was one of the reasons we picked this place.

"Oxford, though?" She turned to me. "Why so far away?"

"It's my dream." She shook her head. "Getting that fellowship has always been a dream. You know that."

"This isn't about that, Corrie, and you know it."

"I know… I just… Why won't you come with me?"

"Because of that. The way you ask. It's like it kills you to even invite me."

She didn't respond, and that was all the answer I needed. I had no fight in me, and she didn't want to fight for me. And though it hurt to let her go, I did it. The reward for doing so was so much better than I'd thought it would be. Elena was so much more than I'd thought I would ever be allowed to have.

After taking a seat in an empty area at my gate, I pulled out my phone and called Elena again.

"Hey, you've reached Elena…"

I gripped my phone tightly and closed my eyes. After taking a few deep breaths, I called Elijah's phone.

"You've reached Elijah Brooks…"

"Fuck," I muttered.

Where are you, Elena?

Next, I tried calling, Nova. The line rang three times, and then she picked up.

"Noah…"

"Nova, what the hell is going on?" I asked. "I've been calling you and Elijah for hours." Her sniffles filled the phone, and my heart dropped. "What's wrong? What is it?"

"Um… Uh… their mom. She's gone, Noah." It took a minute for the words to process in my brain, but when they did, I was no good.

She needed me, and I wasn't there.

"I don't even… How's Elena? Where is she?"

"She's home, Noah," she whispered. "She won't leave her room. Elijah has tried to get her to come out, but she isn't budging, and we don't… we don't know what to do."

"Why didn't anyone call me?"

"Noah, she begged Elijah not to. She said that you needed to work and that she can't have you rushing to her side." She sniffed and then continued. "She's so used to taking care of everyone else, and it doesn't stop. Not even when she's hurting. All she kept saying was to please leave you to your work."

"But she texted me, Nov," I said. "She said she needed me. Why would she—"

"A moment of weakness," she said, cutting in. "We all have them. She loves you, you know? I mean, she really loves you, and I think you're the only person who can pull her out of the darkness she's falling into. Can you get here soon?"

"I'm already on my way."

───

"I JUST LANDED I'm leaving JFK now."

Elijah sighed into the phone, and then he said, "Go home for the night and come here tomorrow." I shook my head as I walked through the airport like a man on a mission. And I was on a mission.

"I need to see her tonight, Elijah."

The thought of coming home to get to her just to wait another day made me sick.

"Noah, she's won't even—"

"She'll open the door for me," I said, not letting him finish his statement. "I know she will. I'm on my way."

"Alright, I'll see you in a minute." His response was one of reluctance, but that didn't matter to me.

"You can leave when I get there," I added, before ending the call.

Nothing would keep me away from her. Not when she was hurting. Not when I know that all she needs is me. Just like all I needed was her.

An hour and a half later, I was entering Elena's building and rushing to her sixth-floor apartment. The elevator ride up felt like an eternity, just as the ride over here in the Uber.

Three minutes.

It took three minutes to get to her door. I knocked once and then again. After the third time, the door swung open, and Elijah stood in front of me. He looked lost. I could feel his pain.

He stepped back, and I walked inside. The apartment was eerily silent. My legs and heart were pulling me toward Elena's bedroom, but instead of moving, I reached for Elijah and pulled my brother-in-law into a tight hug.

"I'm sorry." His arms sagged next to us, and then they wrapped around me. "I don't even—"

"Just make sure she's good," he said, pulling away. "I need to get home to Nova." I nodded and let him out. After locking the door behind him, I made my way toward Elena's bedroom. I knocked but got no answer. I tried turning the knob, but she had it locked. Sighing, I knocked again.

"Go away, Elijah," she mumbled. "I want to be alone."

"Na... it's me." I was met with silence, and when I opened my mouth to speak again, her bedroom door opened.

And there was my baby.

Her hair was wild and sticking all over her head. The beautiful eyes, I'd fallen in love with were red and watery, her cheeks stained with fresh and old tears. I couldn't reach for her fast enough.

"Noah," she choked, rushing into my arms. "I-I... she—"

"Shhh, it's OK, baby," I murmured, wrapping my arms around her. "I'm here. I got you." I maneuvered us into the room and kicked the door shut. I fell back onto her queen-sized bed and pulled her on top of me. She buried her face into my neck and sighed. "You said you needed me, and then you didn't answer."

"I just... you already do so much for me, and I didn't

want…" Her body began to shake in my arms, and I held her tighter. The room filled with her painful cries, and I couldn't find the words to say to make them stop. Her pain was mine now. I'd take it all if it meant that she didn't have to endure it anymore.

A couple of hours later, Elena was lying beside me lightly snoring while I watched her. She was in so much emotional pain that I could see it on her face even while she slept. I turned on my back and stared up at the ceiling. I had no idea how to help her through this, but I would try my best. I knew how much she loved her mother. It didn't matter that she didn't remember her most of the time. She was alive, and that meant the world to Elena. Now that she was gone…

"She passed in her sleep," she whispered through a sleepy haze. "I was almost to the facility when I got the call. Elijah was calling on the other line while I spoke to them, and I felt it in my heart that he was trying to get to me first." I didn't speak. I didn't try to reason that this was God doing what was best. She didn't need that from me, so instead, I turned my body to face hers and gave comfort as best I could. "It hurts, Noah."

"I know, baby." I reached out to wipe away a tear. "Tell me what you need from me."

"I just need you here," she murmured, pressing her face into my hand. "With me. Like this."

"Always."

With pleading eyes trained on me, she asked, "Can you help me forget?" I knew what she meant, but I had no time to respond. Elena slowly sat up and removed the oversized t-shirt that belonged to me, revealing her naked body beneath it. "Please."

She didn't need to beg.

Never needed to.

I pushed her back and climbed between her legs. Leaning forward, I grabbed her face and pressed my lips into hers. The kiss was meant to be soft, but the second we were connected, I lost all resolve. I reluctantly pulled back to shed the rest of my clothes. When she reached out to grab my dick and stroke it, I stopped moving and watched her.

"No foreplay," she said, staring up at me. "I'm already wet for you." She fell back and then spread her legs for me to see. I wanted to taste her. She was dripping right before my eyes, and I wanted to play in it with my tongue, but I wasn't a selfish man. My baby didn't want foreplay, so I gave her what she wanted. Without any warning, I slammed into her. Her pussy locked me in upon impact, and I cursed.

"Please, don't stop," she begged, tears filling her eyes. "I—"

I pulled out and then pushed in, hitting her with a deep stroke. I continued the motion, not letting up. She whispered her love for me while begging me to give her more. I obliged to every request. And I would keep obliging if it meant that she would forget, even if it's only for a little bit.

"Don't ever leave me," she moaned, kissing my lips. "I-I need you."

"I never planned on leaving you, Na," I murmured into her lips. Pausing my strokes to stare at her, I added, "You're mine." I resumed movement with my eyes trained on hers. She was mine, and I wouldn't ever let her get away.

"How is she?" Nova asked, without greeting me. The Uber I rode to my building pulled up to the elevator inside of the parking garage, and I exited. I adjusted my phone on my ear, after grabbing my luggage from the trunk, and then answered Nova.

"She's as good as she can be. I didn't want to leave her, but I needed to drop off my luggage and pack a new bag, and she said she'd be fine while I was gone. I tried convincing her to come with me, but she turned that down. How's Elijah?"

"Quiet," she replied. "Really quiet."

"This is all so fucked up, man." I shook my head and stepped off the elevator onto my floor. As I neared my apartment, I noticed a body leaning up against the wall near my door. The closer I got, the clearer the view became of the person.

"I don't even know what to do and—"

"What the fuck," I mumbled, gaining the person's attention.

"What?" Nova asked. "What's wrong?" I tuned her out and stared at the last person I thought I'd ever see.

"Corrie?" She smiled, and I frowned. This was the last thing I needed right now.

```
┌─────────────────────────────┐
│                             │
│             13              │
│                             │
│            Elena            │
│                             │
└─────────────────────────────┘
```

She was gone, and I didn't get to say goodbye.

What was fair about that?

I was on my way to her. Why couldn't she have waited just a little while longer?

Does that make me selfish?

It was her time, right?

The questions wouldn't stop hitting me. I didn't know what to do. Having Noah beside me for the last twenty-four hours helped, but it didn't stop the questions. My heart shatters into a million pieces every time I think about her being gone. She'd been suffering for a long time, and deep down I know that she's in a better place. But what if she isn't? What if the sin she'd committed all those years ago got her a one way ticket to the place we all feared.

I wiped more tears from my face and buried myself deeper beneath my blanket. No one could have ever prepared me for this type of pain.

"Lena," Elijah called out. He was close. Possibly standing in my bedroom doorway.

"Lijah, I don't know what to do," I cried. Seconds later,

he was pulling the blanket from my body and gathering me into his arms. "W-why did she—"

"It hurts, I know." His voice was shaky, and that made me cry harder. My brother was strong. I don't think I'd ever seen him cry, let alone heard him. "I know we didn't prepare for this, but what can we do besides try to give her the best sendoff that we can."

"She deserves that much," I said, nodding. I took a few deep breaths and then pulled my body away from his to sit up. "Sorry, I locked you out yesterday." He looked over at me and laughed.

"It's all good, I knew what you were feeling." Elijah laid his head back against the wall and closed his eyes. "Noah came through for you."

"Did you call him?' He shook his head, eyes still closed.

"He felt that something was wrong and came on his own. He's good for you." I nodded but didn't speak. He'd proven that to me long ago, but his actions in this instance solidified what I already knew. "I think—" Elijah's phone rang, cutting him off, and he reached for it. While he talked to what I assumed to be Nova, I grabbed my own phone. I hadn't looked at it since finding out about my mom and then texting Noah that I needed him. There were so many text messages from the flower sisters, Brynlee, and co-workers. The message from Magnolia stood out the most.

Magnolia: *Hey, I know this is a tough time for you, and I want to tell you that it'll get better, but truthfully you only learn to live with the pain. The girls and I lost our mom right before I started high school, and it was the most devastating thing I'd ever been through, but I got through it. We all did. You're already an amazing person, Elena. I knew you were special after our first initial meeting, and after getting to know you, I've learned that you're strong and resilient. Pull* *from that strength, and I promise you'll get through this. If you need me, I'm only one call, text, or train ride away. Love ya.*

Magnolia was special. The oldest of five girls and the rock that holds them together. Of course, she would understand what this felt like. I had no idea about them losing their mother, and now that I know, I may take her up on that train ride. I don't want to do this alone, and to know that I have a support system out of this world eases some of the pain.

"Nova, slow down, what are you talking about?"

I glanced at Elijah, and he had a deep frown on his face. He looked my way and then turned his gaze to the bedroom door.

"His ex?" he murmured. "OK. I—Nova, this isn't the time for— alright, alright." He handed me the phone while shaking his head. "She wants to talk to you."

"Hey, Nova, what's wrong?"

"Listen, I was on the phone with Noah while he was headed to his apartment, and when he got there, Corrie was standing outside of his door. He hung up before I could get any more information, and he didn't sound happy to see her but—"

"You just wanted me to know," I finished for her.

"No," she said chuckling. It came out as a strangled noise, and I knew she didn't find what she was saying funny at all. Hell, I didn't either, but what did she want me to do. Noah could handle Corrie. I didn't want to involve myself in that, not now. Not when I had so much more to deal with. "I don't just want you to know, Elena. I want you to go and get your man."

"He's technically not mine," I forced out.

You're mine.

His words from the night before replayed in my mind.

He'd said it, but I was vulnerable, and he was helping me forget.

"Yes, the hell he is," she argued. "She doesn't... You know what, he'll do the right thing. I'm sorry I'm calling you with this bullshit when you're going through so much more. I'm sorry."

"Hey, it's OK," I said. "I get it."

"Just so you know, I'll shoot my own twin for you if he hurts you." I smiled at the seriousness in her tone. Leave it to Nova, to make me smile. "I'll come to see you soon, OK?"

"Today?" I asked. "Can that happen today?" I needed to be surrounded by love.

"Yea, that can happen today." I handed Elijah the phone, and he left the room. I laid back in my bed and tried to process what I'd just been told. Corrie was in town, and she was at Noah's apartment. The bitch had great timing, I'd give her that.

"Hey," Elijah said, poking his head into the room. "I'm heading into the office, and then I'll be back with Nova. Are you going to be good?"

"Yea, I'll be fine." He nodded and walked away. I listened until I heard the apartment door shut and then reached for my phone. I called Noah, and it went to voicemail. I stared at my phone for a few seconds before deciding to send a text.

Me: *Hey, will you be back soon?*

"He won't hurt you," I mumbled to myself. "He said you were his."

I tried coaching away the insecurities. Maybe if I wasn't already in such a horrible emotional state, I would have been able to. Before I knew it, thirty minutes had passed with no reply. I was also dressed and heading out the door. I'd just lost my mother, and I refused to lose Noah too. Not now. Not ever.

I slid into Nova's truck, started it up, and then headed into the direction of Noah's Manhattan apartment.

Life was too short, and we never know when we're going to be taken. Now was the time to tell him how I really felt. I thought the trip to Arizona was it. That the time we'd spent there and the things we'd done were enough to confirm what we both wanted from each other, but I was wrong. He didn't know how I felt. How I really felt. Noah had no idea that I was completely and utterly in love with him.

Now was the time to tell him.

"How will I know when the time is right?"

"When you aren't asking yourself if it's the right time."

Of course, my mother gave the best advice, even in her state at the time. I wasn't second guessing my feelings anymore and refused to second guess what I knew Noah felt for me. Corrie wasn't for him, I was. And I would fight for that because I deserve the happiness he brings me.

Forty minutes later, I was whipping the Benz truck into the parking spot Noah had given to me and then hopping out. I was out of the elevator and on his floor in record time. When I reached his door, I knocked four times and stepped back. A few seconds—that felt like minutes passed —before the door was being pulled opened. I expected to see Noah, but instead, I was met with a pair of hazel eyes that were attached to a woman's beautiful, blemish-free face. I looked her over without speaking. She was gorgeous, and I could see why Noah had fallen in love with her, but she wasn't me.

"Hi," she spoke, bringing my attention to her face. "Are you looking for Noah?" I didn't respond, I just stared at her. Why was she answering his door?

"Corrie, I told you to—"

Noah's deep voice cut out after he moved her out of the way. His anger filled eyes softened as they found mine.

"I wasn't—"

He grabbed my hand and pulled me inside before I could finish my statement.

"Are you OK?" he asked, looking me over with his arms wrapped around my waist. "I was about to be on my way back, but"—he looked at Corrie then back at me— "I had an uninvited visitor."

"Nova called." He smirked as if he'd known she would.

"Of course, she did." He grabbed my hand and pulled us past Corrie. She watched us both intently while I watched her. We moved into the living room, where I spotted his book bag and luggage. "You said you wanted to talk." His eyes were now trained on Corrie. She looked at me and then back at him.

"I was hoping we could talk… alone," she said, glancing at me again. I could feel how threatened she was by my presence from where I was standing. From where she wanted to be standing. It was written all over her face. She came here to try and get him back.

"That's not happening," he replied, shaking his head. "I told you before that now wasn't a good time, but since the reason that now isn't good is here, you can talk. If you don't want to say it in front of her, then it doesn't need to be said." His words were final. Her face told me she understood what he meant, and I was sure mine mirrored hers. He'd said so many things without actually saying them.

"Hey," I said, moving to stand in front of him. "It's OK, I'll go chill out in your room or something."

He shook his head and said, "That's not necessary, Na."

"I love you." I decided to give him a different response. I didn't care that Corrie was standing right behind us. She didn't matter in this moment and at all for that matter.

"I know, and you need—"

"No, I'm in love with you," I clarified, reaching up to cup his face. "I have been for a while now, and I was scared to tell you because... for a lot of reasons that don't matter anymore. I came here to tell you that because life is short, and I may never get the opportunity again." His eyes danced across my face. The love I knew he felt for me, shining through. "I have so much more I want to say but—"

"I love you too," he blurted. "I'm in love with you too."

I never knew hearing that would feel so good, but damn did it feel great. I stood on my tiptoes and kissed the corner of his mouth. I leveled myself on the floor again and pulled his head down toward my lips.

"Handle that," I whispered in his ear. I walked away and toward his bedroom without another word or look in Corrie's direction. Once again, she didn't matter.

Noah belonged to me.

Always had.

14

Noah

I WATCHED MY HEART RETREAT TO THE BACK OF MY apartment before turning my attention to the woman who had once held that spot. I didn't think I'd ever see her again, but I should have known better. I let my thoughts get in the way of my knowledge of Corrie as a woman. She couldn't get any information out of my parents, and she knew not to call Nova. She also could have picked up the phone to call me, but she didn't because she knew I wouldn't feed into whatever it is that she was up to.

"Talk," I said, pointing to the seat behind her, while I sat on the couch closest to me. She took a seat on the reclining chair and crossed her legs at the ankle.

"I didn't think you'd move on so fast."

"It's been almost a year."

"Ten months, two weeks," she said. I shrugged. Her giving an exact time frame didn't stop it from still almost being a year since she walked out of the door. Out on *us*.

"For what it's worth, moving on had been the furthest thing from my mind, but because it wasn't planned didn't mean it wouldn't happen."

"Being at Oxford has been great," she said, changing subjects. I eyed her curiously and then nodded.

"Glad it's working out."

"I um… I heard Nova got married." I nodded but didn't reply. "And she's pregnant."

"You know an awful lot about my sister's life." A guilty expression flashed across her face but was gone quickly after that. "I take it you and Sloane still talk."

"From time to time."

Laughing, I said, "You mean you call her for information, and she gives it but only because she thinks you genuinely care."

Sloane is me and Nova's cousin on our father side. She lives in Philly and has all of her life, but she spent enough summers with us in New Jersey for her and Corrie to know who each other were.

"I do care," she argued. "I just knew you wouldn't tell me anything."

"Corrie, why are you here?" She opened her mouth, but I cut in to add, "And please don't give me any bullshit about you coming to see how I was. I won't believe for one second that you came all of this way just for that."

"I guess I thought…" She glanced toward the back and then down at her hands.

"You thought what?" I pushed. I was ready to get this conversation over with. Elena needed me, and that was all I could think of. "That you could show up, and things would go back to how they were." She looked away, and I laughed. "Oh, I get it. You heard about Elena."

"I didn't think you would be in love, but I was wrong," she whispered, bringing her gaze back to mine. "She makes you happy." I nodded. "And I can see that there wouldn't be a chance for you and me again."

"I don't think you came here because you want us together again, Corrie."

She didn't have to answer for me to know that I was right. Corrie didn't want me. She didn't want an *us*. What she wanted was to still have a part of me, even if that meant getting information from wherever she could get it. That still didn't tell me why she'd come. She hadn't hopped on that fourteen-hour flight just for me.

"My sister had her baby," she blurted as if she were reading my mind. "And I figured I'd drop by to see you while I was in town."

"I appreciate you coming by," I said, standing. "But now really isn't a good time for this. I think we've established where we stand and maybe some time down the line we can sit and have a conversation but now—"

"Isn't the time… right." She stood and followed me to the door. After stepping out into the hallway, she turned to face me. "I'm glad that you're happy, Noah."

"I hope you are too," I said. I watched her until she disappeared on the elevator and then shut the door. Watching her walk away wasn't the same as it had been ten months ago. I didn't feel that pain in my chest that I had before. The fear I felt about not being worthy of Elena's love wasn't there either. She told me she loved me. That she was in love with me just twenty-four hours after her mother passed. She said it right in front of the woman who I'd once felt that way for. Elena was… she was everything.

"Is she finally gone," her raspy voice asked. I'd noticed the change in it when she stood out in the hallway trying to talk. All the crying she'd done put a strain on her usual soft tone.

"Yea, baby, she's gone." I moved toward her with my arms open. She wasted no time walking right into my embrace. "Did you really come all the way here to tell me that you loved me?" She laughed.

"Not initially. I had called and then texted you, but when you didn't respond, I decided to just come over."

"To put claim on what's yours?" She pressed her chin into my chest and stared up at me.

"Yea, something like that." Her eyes watered, and she shut them. "On the way here, I thought about a conversation I had with my mom. I was telling her that I was in love with you and I didn't know what to do, and she said to me that I didn't need to rush things. That I would know the right time to tell you, and it hit me as I was driving. Now was that time. It took her…" She opened her eyes and gave me a watery grin. "It took her being taken away from me for me to see that I couldn't let that happen with us. I'm not afraid anymore."

I kissed her forehead while I pulled her hair from the loose bun she had it in.

"I like it better when you wear it down," I said, sticking my fingers through her tangled curls to get a good grip. "And for the record, I'm not afraid anymore either. Like you said, life is too short, right?"

"Right." I leaned in for a kiss and then led her to the bedroom.

"Are you sure we should've left them alone?" Nova asked, staring down at her phone. I reached over the table and snatched it from her hand. "Noah—"

"They're fine, Nov," I said, sticking her phone in my pocket. A few days have passed since they learned about their mom, and it took a lot for me to drag Nova away from Elijah. We were only two blocks away from them having lunch while they finished up some things for their mother's funeral. We'd already been to the assisted living facility to clean out her apartment, and that was a lot for both Elijah and Elena. "They have each other."

"Right." She sipped on her drink. "Sometimes, I forget."

I laughed.

"No, you don't." She rolled her eyes and glanced around the diner.

"This place reminds me of that diner we used to frequent in Jersey during the summers." I looked around and nodded.

"Yea, it does," I agreed. "Those were some good times."

"Back when we had no worries in the world."

"Do we have worries now, though?" She stared with a thoughtful guise on her face. We were blessed to come from parents who were well off but didn't coddle us. They taught us that hard work was the only way to make it out here.

"I guess when you really think about it, we don't," she finally answered. "Just real life things that we have no control over."

"Exactly," I said. "We have everything we need. Friends who are genuine and love that's real. We have it good."

She smiled.

"So you and Elena aren't *just* friends anymore?"

"Nah." I shook my head and sliced my hand through the air. "That's dead. She's mine."

"And you love her?"

"I'm *in* love with her," I corrected. "She'll be my wife one day."

"I'm happy for you, Noah. You deserve someone like her. She compliments you well."

I couldn't have agreed more.

She was my other half.

I'd never been so sure about something in my entire life until she came into it. I wasn't sure I'd ever be able to love again. Love is a fire. But whether it is going to warm your heart or burn down your house, you can never tell. My house may have been burned down before, but not this time. Not with Elena.

"Can I have my phone?" Nova asked with a mouthful of French fries. The waiter had brought out our order not that long ago, and she'd damn near devoured her plate. I handed over her phone and reached for my own. I scrolled through the notifications and then opened the text from Elena.

Elena: *This is so stressful.*

Me: *Do you need me?*

Elena: *Yes, but no. I need to do this with just Elijah. We are almost finished at the funeral home. Did you guys find food?*

I wanted to go to her, but I had to respect her wishes at the same time.

Me: *A diner a couple of blocks away. I planned on ordering you something to go.*

Elena: *Elijah said we'll meet you guys there once we are done. Nova sent your location.*

I glanced at my sister, who was grinning down at her phone and shook my head.

"They're going to—"

"Meet us here," I finished. "I know." She nodded and reached over to grab my half-eaten burger off my plate.

"You weren't going to finish this, were you?' she asked, biting into it.

"I was, but since you're pregnant and I love you, I won't make a big deal out of you stealing it." She smirked and bit into the burger again.

After about thirty minutes, Elijah and Elena came walking into the diner, looking exhausted. Elena's eyes found mine immediately. She tapped Elijah and pointed our way. As they made their way over, I watched her intently. She looked so tired and down. I was so used to seeing her with bright eyes and a big smile on her face. I needed to figure out a way to get her back to that.

"Hey, baby," she greeted, sliding into the booth next to me. I turned slightly to wrap my arms around her, and she buried herself deep into my embrace. "You smell so good." I pulled her closer and kissed her forehead.

"Hey," Elijah said, as he and Nova both slid out of the booth. "We're going to head out, but I'll see you tomorrow." Elena nodded and then turned her attention back to me after they walked away.

"You good?" She shook her head.

"I would like to leave, too," she murmured. "I'm tired."

Pushing her hair out of her face, I stared into her eyes.

"Do you want to at least order something to go?" She'd barely been eating these last few days, and even my usual persuasion wasn't working.

"No, thank you." She gave me those pleading eyes I couldn't say no to, and I did what she wanted.

"My place or yours?" I asked once we were inside of my truck.

"Yours." She tucked her legs underneath her body, leaned her head back against the headrest, and then closed her eyes. "I don't want to be alone." I reached over, grabbed her hand, and intertwined our fingers together.

She'd never have to be alone as long as I was around. For as long as she allowed, I would have her back. I kissed the back of her hand and then headed into the direction of my apartment.

"I love you," she murmured.

"I love you too, Na."

```
┌─────────────────────────────────┐
│                                 │
│               15                │
│                                 │
│             Elena               │
│       TWO WEEKS LATER...        │
│                                 │
└─────────────────────────────────┘
```

"ELENA, BABY, YOU HAVE TO EAT," MY AUNT FUSSED. I stared at her as she moved effortlessly around my room, picking up clothes and tossing them into a laundry basket. I really didn't understand why she was still here in New York. I love my aunt, I really do, but she'd been working my last nerve. She came for the funeral, which was a week ago, and she was still here. I truly wished that she would go back home to Detroit and bother me through text or something. I wanted to grieve how I saw fit. Not based on the standards of how anyone else believes I should be. Everyone else seemed to understand that, but not Hera.

I rolled my eyes as she moved closer to my bed with that damn basket perched up on her hip. I was getting flashbacks from my teenage years that was making my skin crawl.

"When are you going to go see your father?"

"When I feel like it." Hera was my father's older sister. They were the dynamic duo that gave their neighborhood hell back in their day. I used to love hearing the stories about Hera shutting down the block because she was fighting and beating up everyone in sight. She still had that feistiness to her.

"You got that man to agree to let you go, and then you bail on him." She shook her head as if she were disappointed, and I laughed.

"Hera, please mind your business," I said. "What I decide to do when it comes to *my* father is *my* business, not yours. When are you going home?"

There was fire in her eyes, and I knew she wanted to give me hell, but I was ready for it. She didn't have a say in how I handled any of this. I knew my father was hurting that they denied him coming to the funeral, and I felt for him, I really did, but I was still hurting too. I didn't want to see him inside of that place like that, not now. Not after seeing my mother in a casket. It would only add to the pain that I'm harboring. I also was dreading the bomb; he wanted to drop on Elijah and me. I just wasn't ready for any of it.

I was surprised when my aunt backed down without a fight.

"I booked a flight this morning for later tonight," she said, turning her back to me. "Elena, I know you're hurting, and I know you feel as though the pain will never go away, but it will. You just have to fight *it* and not everyone else. That man you love, you remember him, right? The one who you've been gradually pushing away, he won't wait around forever. He loves you that I can tell, but it's only so much he'll take from you. Get it together." She walked away, shutting the door behind her.

I tried not to think about what she'd just said. I tried so hard to push it away, but I couldn't. How could I?

Noah meant the world to me, but seeing him or anyone for that matter made me feel like I had to get over my mother's death for their sake, and I wasn't ready. I didn't want to move on. I wanted her back.

I thought that I would have wanted all the support I was getting, but it was overwhelming. I needed to be left alone for a while. I just… needed a minute to get my mind right.

"Hello." I'd answered my phone without looking. I knew who it was already.

"Let me take you to lunch," he said. He was straight forward this time. No asking me how I was or if I needed anything. Those two questions were driving me insane.

"I could eat," I replied, walking into my bathroom. I looked into the mirror but only briefly. I hadn't been liking what I was seeing lately. Sad eyes with heavy bags under them were a part of my everyday look now. It was pathetic, but I didn't have the energy to care. "Should I meet you or—"

"I'll come scoop you in an hour." He ended the call before I could respond.

I set my phone on the counter and stripped out of the baggy t-shirt—that belonged to Noah—and my underwear. I cut on the shower and set the temperature to my liking and then stepped inside. The hot water beat against my skin, and I hummed in pleasure. I needed this. A good shower always clears the mind, or in my case, it helps me think more clearly.

The last few weeks have been a roller-coaster ride from hell. Elijah has completely buried himself in a case, and the only person he will talk to is Nova. I can't blame him or even judge because I've been worse. I should have been taking a page out of his book and leaning on Noah more. Don't get me wrong I wanted to do that, but I also didn't want to feel like my pain was becoming his. I didn't want to feel better one day and then look at him just to see that he was drained. I didn't know how he was truly feeling about my behavior, but I had an idea. I could see it on his face when I couldn't find it in me to engage in conversation with him. It wasn't that I didn't want to, my mind just wouldn't let me get past the fact that my mother was never coming back.

Was I depressed, or was this just a phase?

I'd managed to go back to work and get through a shift without running off to cry in the bathroom. I'd also managed to eat an entire meal a few days ago without throwing it up afterward. Maybe I was getting better, or maybe I was psyching myself out so that I wouldn't get better.

You're a fucking mess, Elena.

Instead of dwelling on my inner thoughts, I washed my body, rinsed, and then got out of the shower. I didn't get dressed up. I just put on a pair of distressed blue jeans and my black Nike hoodie. By the time I was finished throwing my hair into a top knot, I heard Noah's voice in the apartment.

"I'm good, how are you?" his deep baritone asked. The sound was like music to my ears and a shock to my heart. I couldn't hear my aunt's response, but I knew she was giving him the rundown of how I'd been acting when I'm not in his presence. I took a few more minutes to put on my sneakers and then gathered an overnight bag. After finishing, I tossed it over my shoulder, grabbed my purse and phone, then headed toward the living room.

"Hey," I said, entering the room. Noah turned his head to look me over, and I did the same with him. He was dressed down just as casual as I was. Dark jeans, black Adidas hoodie, and the sneakers to match. Our moods were definitely giving off the same vibes today.

"Hey, are you ready?" he asked, moving toward me.

He looked at my overnight bag and then back at me. "I get you for the night?" He took the bag from my hands as I nodded.

"Yea, if that's OK."

"It always is." I gave a quick smile and then turned my attention to my aunt, who was pretending not to watch us. I slowly walked toward her, and the second I was in arms reach, she grabbed me.

"I love you, little lady," she whispered into my ear. "Don't you ever forget that."

"I know," I replied, tightening my arms around her. "I love you too."

"Good." We broke our embrace, but I stayed rooted in my spot.

"Call me when you make it back home." I already knew that Elijah would get her to the airport. He may have been checked out, but he'd already told her when she was ready to go that he'd take her.

"Of course." I nodded and then turned to meet Noah at the front door. "Elena?"

"Yes?"

"If you ever call me Hera again, be ready to square up." I glanced over my shoulder at her with a wide smile on my face. There was that fight she wanted earlier but didn't push for. I knew she wouldn't let me get away with calling her Hera, and when I was in my right mind, I will call and apologize for the disrespect.

"I love you too, auntie."

"Mmhm," was her response to me and Noah's retreating backs.

Noah grabbed my hand as we walked toward the elevators.

"She's something else," he said, making small talk.

"Been that way my whole life." I leaned my head on

his arm and sighed. "Where are we eating?"

"Corner Bistro." My stomach growled.

"My favorite."

"I figured it might help make you feel a little better," he said, as we reached his truck. I looked his way and was met with his intense gaze. "I'll do anything to help get that sparkle back in your eyes." Not being able to take it anymore, I looked away and then slid into the passenger seat. Noah was good at saying the sweetest things. He was also good at proving that he meant what he said.

The drive to Corner Bistro was quiet but comfortable. Rod Wave's album Ghetto Gospel played softly in the background. How Noah knew that I'd basically been listening to it nonstop the last few days was beyond me, but I liked that he had it playing. I bobbed my head to the song Dark Conversations.

He havin' conversations in the dark, yeah, yeah
It's just me, myself, and my heart, uh
My heart said, "under any circumstance or for any reason
Lay down your guard again and I'ma stop beatin'
Please, friend, I cannot take it no more

The song spoke to me. There were some parts of the lyrics that I didn't resonate with, but when he talks about the man having conversations in the dark. How it's four in the morning, and everyone else is asleep, but he's wide awake with his thoughts riding him hard, I felt that. I felt it to my core. Recently I've had so many dark conversations in the dead of night. I'm not proud of my thoughts, but they're there, and sometimes they are hard to get rid of.

"What's on your mind?" Noah asked, reaching for my hand. I gave it up without a fight. He laced our fingers together and rested them on the middle console.

"Everything." He was silent for a while, and I thought he'd taken my answer for what it was.

But then he said, "When you want to let me back in, I'll be here." And what he did next, warmed my heart. He didn't wait for an answer. I don't even think he expected one. He kissed the back of my hand and turned the music up. It dawned on me then that he was giving me space while still being there for me. My Aunt Hera was wrong. Noah wouldn't be pushed away easily. It would take more than a tragedy and me shutting down for him to walk away.

I didn't want him to walk away. I wanted him. I just wanted... *him*.

And I couldn't be sure when these raw feelings would subside, or if they ever will, but I knew when I was ready to come back that he would be there to pull me out of my dark thoughts.

I glanced over at Noah and watched as he mouthed the lyrics to the song Cuban Links featuring Kevin Gates. He seemed so content with us being just as we are. I knew he wasn't. I knew my actions lately had to be hurting him. I didn't want that. I really didn't.

Don't take him for granted.

I grimaced and looked away.

Was I already taking him for granted?

```
┌─────────────────────────────────┐
│                                 │
│               16                │
│                                 │
│             Noah                │
│                                 │
└─────────────────────────────────┘
```

I watched Elena pretend to be sleep. I knew just from how uneven her breathing was that she was wide awake, but she didn't want me to know. She didn't want me to ask questions. She also didn't want me to bear her pain. There was nothing she could really do about that, but I would let her think she could.

"I can feel how heavy your thoughts are," I said, pulling her body closer to mine.

"Sorry," she mumbled, opening her eyes. "Did I wake you?"

"I was never asleep."

I let the silence she wanted fill the space around us again. I didn't want to push too hard because I knew she wasn't ready to let go yet. I also didn't want to be lax about it because letting her fall too deep wasn't an option. Allowing that would mean me eventually having to let her go. That wasn't an option for me. It wasn't an option for *us*.

Her aunt tried giving me advice on how I should deal with Elena, but I wouldn't take it. Hera was a different type of tough, and she dished that out without any thought. I admired her but not enough to actually give Elena an ultimatum. It would never, ever, come to that. I knew in my heart that she would never let it come to that. When soft snores fell from her lips, I smiled. She'd finally given in to it. I leaned in and kissed her forehead and then her lips before removing myself from bed and heading to my office. While she slept, I could get some work done.

I was only about thirty minutes into checking my emails when my phone rang. When I saw that it was Elijah calling, I answered and then placed it on speaker.

"Yo."

"Is Elena good?" he asked. "My aunt said she was a little on the snappy side today."

"She's good."

"Is she still quiet?"

"The same as you are." He chuckled.

"Touché."

Elijah wanted his sister to be back to herself already when he wasn't even there himself. They both had that, *I want to take care of everyone but myself,* nature about them. It was a little annoying, but it was what it was.

"Have you asked her about seeing our pop?" he asked.

"Why is it that everyone wants *me* to ask her?"

"Because she'll be susceptible to you asking versus any of us."

"Even you?"

I didn't understand what the rush was. She didn't need to go see him if she wasn't ready, and I didn't plan on trying to force her.

"I mean… yea, even me."

"Look," I paused and rubbed a hand down my face. "I'll think about bringing it up, but not anytime soon."

"Bring what up?" Elena asked, leaning up against the

door frame of my office. I hung up on Elijah and leaned back in my seat. She had weary eyes trained on me.

"It's not important," I said. "Come here."

She slowly walked toward me and then sat in my lap. I wrapped an arm around her waist and pulled her close.

"You weren't sleep long."

"You weren't there when I reached for you."

"Sorry about that."

She was looking at everything but me, and the shit was bothering me. Instead of letting her do it, I gripped her chin and turned her to face me.

"Na, talk to me." Her eyes filled with tears, and I regretted asking. I couldn't take her crying on me. It was painful to watch and hearing it… hearing her cries… that fucked with my heart, man.

"I-I… it just hurts still, and I don't know how to make it stop."

"Let me help," I mumbled into her mouth before sealing the statement with a kiss. I didn't linger as long as I'd liked. Instead, I kissed away the tears that fell freely from her eyes. "I love you beautiful. I know you feel down right now and a little helpless, but I'm here. I'm right here. All you have to do is lean on me." I kissed her lips again, and when she deepened it, I took that as a win. A small one, but a win, nonetheless. "Let me take care of you."

She adjusted her body to straddle me in the chair and then wrapped her arms around my neck.

"Thank you for being patient with me," she murmured, grinding into my erection. "I know I've been difficult." I shook my head and lifted her face. She slowly brought her down, casted gaze to mine.

"Not difficult," I started, kissing her lips. "You're griev-ing, and everyone does it differently."

"I want to feel you inside of me."

I didn't waste any time moving us from the chair to the couch I had inside of my office. On the way, I stepped out of my basketball shorts. The second I had us lowered onto the couch, Elena was sliding down onto me. She was soaked and whimpering from the invasion.

"Tell me what you want."

"Slow," she murmured. "Make love to me."

I flipped us so that she was on her back and buried myself deeper inside of her. She wanted slow, so that was what I gave her. At this point, I would give Elena any and everything she wanted to make her feel better.

"I-I love you," she moaned, digging her nails into my back.

"I love you more beautiful."

"WHAT DID Elijah want you to talk to me about?"

I glanced over my shoulder at her and then focused my attention back on the pork chops I was braising. It had been a successful day so far, and a part of it had to do with her letting go in my office the way that she had. What I didn't want to do was say something that would send her back into her shell. Not when I'd finally gotten a piece of her back. She'd even been smiling and laughing. The actions actually meeting her eyes.

"Not anything important enough to bring up right now," I answered, turning to face her. She stared at me curiously while chewing on the cotton candy grapes she loved so much. I kept the fridge stocked with them just for her.

"Noah—"

"It's not important," I stated again. Her brows furrowed, and she looked away from me. "I want you to focus on this moment, Na. What everyone else wants doesn't matter right now."

"Yea, but… I'm not fragile, Noah."

I frowned.

"No, but you're a little snappy when it comes to certain things, and I'd rather not bring that out of you."

"I don't mean to be that way," she said. "I want people to treat me like they used to."

"You can't want that, but then get upset when things are brought up that you don't want to discuss."

"How is that different from any other time?" she asked, tone hard.

"Elena, you're the sweetest person I've ever met. And though you have some fire to you, it's never to the point that you're being disrespectful."

"I see Hera got you on her side." I chuckled.

"Don't let her hear you say that." She rolled her eyes and stuffed a few grapes into her mouth. "I'd hate to see you get beat up."

"I'm not scared of her."

"You don't need to be scared to get beat up, Na." Laughter filled the kitchen, and I didn't think anything had ever sounded so good. Elena glanced my way, and I saw a glimpse of the old her. It was a nice sight.

"Please," she quipped, smiling. "Hera can't keep up with me. Maybe back in the day, but not now."

Laughing, I turned toward the stove and started making gravy from scratch. I was preparing smothered pork chops and rice for dinner. It was one of my favorite things to eat and cook.

"You can tell me, I would never snap on you," she said, taking us back to the previous conversation. "It's probably why he asked you."

"His words exactly," I mumbled, adding water to the

flour and whisking. "He wants to know when you'll be ready to see your dad." As my gravy began to thicken, I dropped some beef bouillon cubes into it for flavor. I let it boil and then dropped the braised pork chops into the gravy and lowered the temperature. They would simmer for about an hour and be falling off the bone just as I liked it. After covering the pan, I turned around and moved toward Elena. She hadn't responded to what I said, but I knew she wouldn't right away.

"I'm not ready," she said, handing me some grapes. "Why do they want to force it."

"Truthfully, I don't think Elijah cares one way or another. It was Hera who seems to be pushing for it."

"I figured." She sipped on her water with her eyes trained on me. "It's only because she knows what he has to say."

"Maybe it isn't bad, Na."

"I didn't get the vibe that it was anything good."

"Is any news good besides, *Hey, I'm being released early?*"

Her shoulders dropped, and she sighed.

"I guess you are right."

"I could be wrong too, but I'm playing devil's advocate."

"Always looking at things from every perspective."

Chuckling, I ran my fingers through her curls and said, "It's who I am."

"I love who you are," she moaned, leaning her head into my fingers. I took the hint and massaged her scalp.

"I love who you are, even more, Na."

"I'll see if Elijah is available to see him this weekend."

I moved behind her and buried my face into her neck.

"You don't have to go if you aren't ready." I placed soft kisses along her shoulder while sliding my hands up her shirt. She sank into my embrace, and it brought a smirk out of me. No matter what was happening, she always reacted beautifully to my touch.

"I'll probably…" her words trailed as I softly began to run the pad of my thumbs over both nipples. "P-Probably never be ready, so I just need to do it."

"I'll go with you then." She tilted her head back slightly to look at me.

"I thought I would want to say no, but I'd like you to come."

I was pleased with that response, and instead of responding with words, I went in for a kiss.

"Do we have time to—"

I lifted her into my arms bridal style, cutting her off. I knew where her statement was going, and I was all for it.

"It's on a low simmer," I said. "We have time."

LAUGHTER AND THE SMELL OF BACON PULLED ME FROM MY sleep about forty-five minutes ago. I knew the voices well, so I took my time showering and getting dressed before emerging from Noah's bedroom. He'd kissed me goodbye a few hours prior, but I'd missed where he said he was going.

"Oh, she's finally alive," Brynlee chimed, walking over to me. She pushed a plate into my hands and then guided me to the table. "Sit and eat." I cut an eye at Nova, but she ignored me by staring down into her phone.

"Um… what's going on?" I asked, after biting into a piece of bacon.

"We're going dress shopping," Brynlee answered. She sat next to me with a cup of what I was assuming was tea. Noah didn't drink coffee, and he didn't keep any in his apartment. "I found the perfect shop, and I finally have my colors just right."

"And?" I piled some eggs and home fries onto my fork and stuffed my mouth.

"Royal, blue and purple." I nodded while swallowing down my food.

"Good choice. Those two colors together are gorgeous."

"I agree," Nova said, joining the conversation. She walked past me, snatching a piece of my bacon along the way. I rolled my eyes, and she laughed.

Patting her small baby bump, she said, "This little one likes bacon."

"Don't blame your obsession with bacon on my god, baby," Brynlee joked. "Anyway. We have an appointment at four, and the—" Loud knocks on the door cut her out.

"They're here," Nova sang.

"Who?"

Brynlee smiled but didn't answer.

"I smell bacon, so I hope there's more," Juniper yelled. Her voice was the most distinctive of them all. A smile slowly stretched across my face as the rest of the flower sister voices filled the apartment. They began to file into the kitchen, and Blossom was on me before I could even open my mouth to speak.

"Hey, pretty," she whispered, hugging me tightly. She didn't need to say more for me to understand what the hug meant. And man did I appreciate the silent vow of support.

"Move." Magnolia pushed Blossom aside and then pulled me from my chair.

"Sorry, we couldn't be here for—"

"Don't you dare apologize for that," I said, shaking my head. I looked from her to the others. "None of you."

"But we—"

"You guys have businesses and careers. Trust me, I understand more than you know, and besides, your calls and texts were enough."

"We don't agree," Lilac said, speaking for them all. "But, we won't push it."

I felt really loved in this moment, and it was a good feeling.

"Yo, where's the bacon?" Everyone looked at Juniper, who was searching high and low.

"Aint no more," Brynlee said, laughing. "I didn't think you'd guys would get here for another couple of hours." Juniper's frown deepened.

"I'm confused on what that has to do with the bacon."

Laughing, I slid my plate to her. There were two pieces left, and I wouldn't eat them anyway.

"See, I knew you were my favorite for a reason." A series of lip smacks and eye rolls came from the rest of the sisters, and I smiled. Each sister loved being the favorite, and they argued about it all the time. I personally didn't have a favorite. They were all so different, and truthfully it balanced them out. I connected with each for specific reasons.

"Now that the bacon whore has what she wants, I have a question." That was daisy speaking. She sashayed over to one of the bar stools and sat down. Her light brown eyes sparkled mischievously, and I knew what was coming. "I heard someone might be pregnant."

All eyes landed on Brynlee, who just simply rolled her eyes.

"Nope," she said. "I'm not pregnant. I took six tests at Samir's request and even went to the doctor."

"Mmm," I hummed.

"I'm just stressed about the wedding."

"For what?" I asked. "You guys are already married. The ceremony is just a formality for everyone else."

"Yea, but it's still a wedding, and I want it to be perfect."

"How is it that you're stressed about a wedding that's four months away but executed planning Nova's with a two-week time frame?" Blossom asked, laughing. "A bomb ass wedding might I add."

"Make it make sense," Daisy tacked on.

"They have a point," I added. "Don't worry about pleasing everyone else. Do what you want."

Everyone started added in their two cents, and it felt good to be around people who weren't worried about my state of mind for a change. This was what I needed, and I had a feeling that Noah had something to do with it. As if he knew I were thinking about him, my phone vibrated with a text from him.

Noah: *Don't let those hoodlums named after plants eat me out of a house and home.*

Me: *Too late. Juniper is currently making bacon after complaining about Brynlee not making her any and then eating my last.*

I looked around the kitchen.

Me*: Oh, and Daisy is making a protein shake.*

When a facetime call came through from him, I laughed.

"Yes, Noah."

"Turn the phone around." Laughing, I purposely turned it to face Daisy.

"Daisy, put my shit back," he yelled.

At this point, I was in tears. Noah was serious about his nutrition, but so was Daisy. She always raided his kitchen against his wishes when she was here. She mostly did it because she knew it drove him crazy.

"Oh, quit whining," she said, dumping another scoop into the blender. "You buy the good stuff, and you have enough money to buy more."

"I swear you and your sisters work my nerves more than Nova."

"Hey!" Nova yelled. "Be nice to me, I'm pregnant."

The blender started, and I slipped out of the kitchen to find a quiet place while the girls continued to make themselves more than at home.

"You asked them to come?" He nodded.

"I hope that's cool. I know you've been—"

"It's exactly what I needed," I interjected. "Thank you."

"I got you." He glanced at something in front of him and then shook his head. "Samir has us getting fitted at Loke's shop in Jersey. We'll probably chill out here for a while, so I'll see you later tonight."

"OK, baby."

"Are you staying with me again."

"Yes, I prefer your bed," I said, leaning against his desk. "I'll make a stop at my apartment to grab a few more things."

"Just clean out a drawer and leave some stuff at my place, so you don't have to keep going back and forth."

"I—"

"Don't say whatever it is you're about to say, Na."

"I was just going to say that I'd like that."

He chuckled and said, "Yea, OK."

He knew I was about to be on some bullshit, and I'm glad he stopped me.

"I love you."

"I love you more," he replied. "I'll see you tonight." We hung up, and I smiled. I was beginning to feel normal again. I guess I didn't need to be alone after all.

"There you are," Brynlee mused, leaning against the door frame. "You good?"

For once, I didn't need to think about it.

"Yea, I'm good."

"Great, we are about to head out."

"I thought the appointment wasn't until four."

"It isn't." She shrugged. "We have a spa appointment."

"A spa—never mind, let's go."

I wouldn't fight it. This was all Noah's doing, and I should have known there was more to it. He'd said that he wanted to put the sparkle back in my eyes, and it just might be working.

———

BRYNLEE PULLED into the parking garage of Noah's building and parked in my spot. We all rode in Nova's truck because it had three rows and fit us all inside comfortably.

"What are we doing now?" I asked as we all got out.

"We are going back to Philly," Magnolia answered. I pouted, and she laughed. "We'll see you again soon." She hugged me, and then the other's did the same before they headed for their car.

"I'm heading home," Nova chimed. "A bath is calling my name."

"I'm dropping her off and heading home myself."

My pout turned into a frown. I didn't want the night to be over yet. Noah was still in New Jersey and wouldn't be back for another couple of hours. Being alone didn't sound appealing at all. Today had been such an amazing day. The spa was relaxing, dress shopping was a task, but lunch was nothing but laughs. It was the most fun I'd had in weeks.

"Well... OK." I knew I sounded like a brat, but I didn't

care. "Are you guys sure you don't want to come up and chill for a little while longer?"

"We're sure." Brynlee nodded in agreeance with Nova, and I sighed. "Don't look so sad. We have a dinner date for tomorrow, remember?"

"Right, I almost forgot." Deciding that was good enough, I hugged them goodbye and then headed up to Noah's apartment. Once I reached his door, I used the key he'd left for me and entered. I frowned when the strong smell of lavender, and… food hit me. Food had definitely been cooked, and that's when I realized what was happening.

"Noah," I called out, walking further into the apartment.

"Kitchen, Na," he called back.

I walked into the open space, and what I found melted my heart. Noah was leaning against the island counter with an apron on that said, *I Sell Art… But I Cook A Little Too.* He was holding a bowl filled with strawberries and grinning at me like a fool.

A handsome fool.

I couldn't stop the smile that spread across my face when I spotted the candlelit dinner sitting on the table. Both meals were covered with a silver top, but I had an idea about what he had cooked for me.

"You played me," I said, stepping closer to him. "Can I have one of those?" I loved strawberries, just as much as I did cotton candy grapes. He reached into the bowl and held one out to me.

"Come here, baby," he said, beckoning me. I moved closer, and he lifted the strawberry to my mouth. I bit into the sweet fruit and moaned. "Is it that good?" I ignored him and finished off the berry.

"So good." He set the bowl down and pulled me into his body. "What is all of this?"

"It's me appreciating you."

"Inviting the flower sisters down and the spa day was a part of that too?" He shrugged.

"That was to give you a day to forget. This…"—he waved his hand toward the table— "…is to show my appreciation." I looked away from him.

"I don't deserve this." I tried removing myself from his embrace, and after a few seconds, he allowed it.

"How about you tell me why you feel that way, and I'll tell you why you're wrong."

"I haven't been good to you these last couple of weeks. I've been taken your patience for granted." He chuckled.

"Is that what you think?" I nodded and wiped my eyes. I didn't want to start crying. "Elena, you can't really believe that a couple of weeks of you grieving is enough to make me feel taken for granted?" He shook his head. "God forbid something happens to my parents, but if it were one of them, I wouldn't be standing right now. You may not see your progress, but I do."

Noah reached out and pulled me back to him. He tilted my head up with his index finger and then leaned in to kiss my lips. The sweet invasion did it for me. I decided to let go and enjoy what he'd done for me.

"Are there any other reasons you feel like you don't deserve to be treated like a queen by your man?"

"I—my man?" I asked, giving him my full attention. We'd never talked about making this an official thing. I guess it didn't need to be said, but then again, I liked having the reassurance of what we were. "Are we—"

"Together?" he finished. "I thought that was without saying, but that's my mistake for not making it clear enough for you." He kissed me again and then pulled back. "Will you be my girl?"

"Depends," I said, smiling. He lifted a bushy brow and crossed his arms.

"On what?"

"On what's under those lids." I nodded my head into the direction of the food, and he chuckled. "If it's salmon, then I'll be yours and possibly marry you one day."

"And if I made your favorite dessert, can I get a couple of kids too?"

My eyes widened, and he threw his head back, letting out a deep rumble of laughter.

"If it's what I think it is, then yea. My vagina can handle about three kids."

"Three and a possible, and we have a deal." He stretched his hand out for me to shake, and I took it.

"Deal."

After shaking on it and then sealing it with a kiss, he guided me over to the table. I took my seat and wasted no time unveiling what was on the menu. The smile I was already wearing broadened. He'd gone all out by making the honey glazed salmon I loved so much, along with asparagus, and loaded garlic mash potatoes. I picked up some asparagus and popped it into my mouth. Groaning, I looked over at him and smiled. It was just right.

"You could've been a chef, you know?" I cut into the flaky salmon and stuffed a hefty portion into my mouth. Nodding, I added, "Definitely a chef." He laughed and then dug into his own plate of food. We ate in a comfortable silence, and I had to admit once again that I was feeling a little better.

18

Noah

"ARE YOUR EYES CLOSED!" ELENA YELLED FROM BEHIND THE closed bathroom door. I cut my eyes at the door and then closed them. After dinner, Elena bolted from the table and said she had a surprise for me. She'd been hiding in the bathroom for the last twenty minutes with said surprise.

"Yea, they're closed."

"OK." There was some shuffling, and then the click of a door filled the air. "Lie back."

"I don't like not being able to see what's happening." She laughed.

"I took that into consideration, which is why you weren't blindfolded," she said. "Now lie back, Noah." I reluctantly did as I was asked. A few seconds passed, and then the weight of Elena's entire body was on me. I reached up and ran my fingers over her thighs.

"Can I look?" I asked when my hand hit what felt like lace.

"Yes."

I opened my eyes and leaned up on my elbows.

"Damn," I mumbled, taking her in. She was rocking

some red lacy lingerie. It was a two-piece. The bra had a choker attached, and the shit was sexy as fuck. I ran my fingers over it and then gripped her neck. "When did you get this?"

"T-today..." Her words trailed as I slipped fingers from my free hand into her bra. She whimpered and closed her eyes. "Um... the bridal shop was attached to a lingerie shop." Her eyes were closed, but I nodded anyway. When I'd told Elena that red was her color, I hadn't thought about seeing her in lingerie. Her skin was... it was beautiful against this red fabric and as bad as I wanted to see it off, the idea of fucking her with it on was more appealing in this moment.

"Do you know how sexy you look in this?"

She opened her eyes and bit down on her lip. They were coated in a shiny gloss and looking juicier than ever. I couldn't resist leaning forward and taking her bottom lip into my mouth. I sucked until all of the gloss was gone, and her lip was swollen.

"Noah—"

"Shhh," I said, flipping us. "Do you want your dessert?" Her eyes danced around the room until they landed on the bowl that was sitting on the nightstand. She glanced back at me, and I smirked.

"Is there ice cream in there too?" I nodded and climbed from between her legs. I shed my jeans and shirt, leaving me in just my boxer briefs. After grabbing the bowl and spoon, I took my position back between her thighs. I scooped an even amount of vanilla ice cream and peach cobbler onto the spoon and then lifted it to her mouth. Her lips wrapped around the utensil, and my dick twitched.

Damn, that was sexy.

"Oh my God," she moaned. "Tastes better than the other times you made it."

"I may have added another ingredient." She opened her mouth for more, but I shook my head. "Go sit up against the headboard." She did as I asked without any questions. "Spread your legs a little." That time she cut her eyes at me, but she still obliged. I handed her the bowl, and she took it.

"Noah—"

"You eat, while I do the same," I said, positioning myself between her legs face first. "I pulled her panties to the side and then pushed my fingers into the garter she was wearing. "Eat." I watched as she dipped the spoon into the bowl and then brought it to her lips before diving in for a taste of my own. I ran my tongue against her slick folds and then settled on her clit. "Mmm." Flattening my tongue over her sensitive bud, I licked until she was squirming. I buried my fingers deeper into the garter to keep her in place. I kept my eyes on her while I feasted. The pleasure stricken faces accompanied by her chomping down on the Crown Royal peach cobbler was better than anything I'd ever seen before.

"Mmm," I hummed, sucking on her clit faster. She tasted fucking amazing.

"S-shittt," she moaned. "Noah, I c-can't…"

I shook my head while slurping up her juices. She was beyond soaked, and it was all over my beard. I continued to eat, not caring that she'd ditched the bowl and was now digging her finger into my head.

"Yes… God, yes!" she whimpered, lifting her hips to feed me more. "I'm going to—" I picked up my pace until she screamed out in pleasure. Her body jerked from the orgasm she was shouting about. She pushed my head away, and I didn't fight her on it. I lifted my head from in between her legs with an accomplished smirk on my face. While she was breathing heavily, I pulled her body down further onto the bed so that her back was completely flat.

"Are you tapping out," I asked, removing my boxers. My dick sprang free, and she licked her lips.

"Hell… no."

"Tell me how you want it?" It was my favorite question to ask her. She had no problem telling me how she liked to take it, and I had no problem giving her what she wanted. At all times. She lifted her head a little and then flipped onto her stomach. She positioned herself with her ass in the air, and her face pressed deep into the bed. "You wanna be fucked hard?"

"Yes, please," her soft voice murmured. I took in the beautiful sight before me and licked my lips. She had the most perfect arch in her back, giving me an insane view of her wet pussy.

"I got you, baby," I replied, gripping my dick. "But first, let me feel your lips."

She pushed herself up and turned to face me with a broad smile on her face. Biting down her lip, she smacked my hand away and replaced it with one of hers. I watched her through a hooded gaze as she slowly stroked me. Her hands were small but effective as fuck. Reaching forward, I slipped my fingers through her wild curls and gripped them tight.

"I got you, baby," she mimicked. And then she spit on my dick and devoured me whole.

"Fuck!" I bit out. My dick was deep in her mouth, pressing at the back of her throat, and she wasn't even gagging. She repeated the motion over and over, letting my dick hit her tonsils and then releasing. I knew Elena was nasty, but this was… this was something else. She sucked up all of the spit and then spit it back. Wrapping her lips around the base of my dick, she sucked. Soft and slow and then fast. Over and over. She repeated it over and over, sending me into a different world. I wouldn't last too much longer, and I tried telling her that.

"Na," I groaned. "I'm about… I'm not ready." I pulled her head back, and she released me with a big smile on her wet lips. "Bend over." She was back in that perfectly arched position in no time, and I was buried deep inside of her soon after.

"Shit," we moaned in unison. Yea, the night was just getting started for us.

"Yo," I answered my phone after stepping out of my bedroom. I didn't want to wake Elena. She'd been sleeping peacefully all morning, and I wanted to keep it that way. After last night, I wasn't expecting her to wake up until late into the afternoon.

"Is that how you answer the phone for your mother?"

"Not usually, but it's ten in the morning, and I know you don't want anything." She laughed.

"Oh, I want something," she mused. "How's Elena?"

I thought about the last couple of days and said, "She's better." My mother and father had met Elena on too many occasions to count. With her being Elijah's sister, it was inevitable that they would meet, but when they started seeing her more and more with just me, they knew something more was there. "Much better," I added.

"A little birdy told me that the two of you are…" she paused and then said, "Exploring something more than just a friendship."

"We're in a relationship," I said, laughing. After grabbing a bottle of water, I headed for the living room and plopped down into my reclining chair.

"Well, then your father and I would like to have you both over for dinner soon."

"Depends on what you cook," I joked. I knew this was coming. They knew Elena as my friend and Elijah's sister, so they never pushed to learn more about her. Now that we've become something more, they would be on my head until I brought her over.

"Noah."

"It'll be soon, ma," I said. "She's better, but everything is still fresh, and then things with her dad are weird, so she needs to handle that."

"What's going on with her father?" my dad asked, cutting in. I should've known he was somewhere close for this call. "Anything we can do to help?"

"I don't think so, pop." My parents had connections, but there was nothing they could do for Samuel.

"Are you sure?" my mom asked. "I could reach out to Brandy." Brandy was Brynlee's mother. Her mother and father both worked for the FBI. They were close to retiring, but they weren't quite there yet.

"Honestly, as much as I would like to intervene, that's not my call." If I were to get Brandy involved, then I would have to tell the entire story, and that wasn't my place. I would never betray Elena in that way. And though, Elijah didn't know that I knew the truth, the same went with him. "But if something changes, then I'll let you guys know." There was a brief silence, and then they both spoke at the same time.

"We're proud of you." I smiled.

"It's always good to hear that from you two." I was blessed with parents who knew how to be successful and still be present in their children's lives. I never felt neglected or ignored when it came to them.

I felt a presence that wasn't there before and glanced over my shoulder to find Elena standing there.

"I love you guys, and I promise I'll bring Elena over for dinner soon."

"I think he's getting rid of us," my dad said, laughing. Elena slowly walked toward me with a smile on her face.

"We love you too," my mom spoke before ending the call. Elena dropped into my lap and laid her head on my shoulder.

"Me not being there next to you, woke you?" I asked, kissing her forehead.

"As always," she murmured. "I also heard talking."

"Sorry about that."

She positioned herself to straddle me and then kissed my lips.

"They invited me to dinner?" I nodded.

"They know we're a couple." She didn't even bat an eye at the confession. Elena loved my parents already. The first time she'd met my mom, and she complimented the heels she was wearing, they were best friends in her eyes.

"And they want the tea?"

Laughing, I said, "Something like that."

"Hey, Noah," she murmured, wrapping her arms around my neck and then resting her head on my shoulder again.

"Yes, baby?"

"Thank you for last night." I kissed her cheek while wrapping my arms around her.

"Which part?"

"Dinner, dessert…" she paused and lifted her head. "And everything after."

"What about everything during?" I asked, lifting my brows suggestively.

She laughed and then said, "That was bomb too."

"There's more where that came from," I said. "I got you always."

She nodded with a content look on her face.

"Is the sparkle back in my eyes yet?" I ran my fingers along her jawline while staring in her eyes.

"I see a little dust of something." Her laughter filled the room again, and I was done for. That laughter was everything my heart would ever need. "I love you."

"I love you too, Noah."

SUNDAY AFTERNOON...

I'd been dreading this, I thought.

My heartbeat against my chest, and it was almost painful to feel. I looked around the gloomy visitation room for the millionth time and grimaced. I couldn't imagine what the rest of the place looked like. This is where my father had been for the last sixteen years. I hadn't physically seen him in sixteen years.

That's one hundred and ninety-two months.

Eight hundred and thirty-four weeks.

Five thousand eight hundred and forty days.

I'd googled that on the drive here. I wanted to know how much time had actually passed and when it's broken down like that, it's more real.

How could he let so much time pass without seeing his daughter?

It couldn't have been easy for him. It was painful for me. Especially being able to hear his voice, but nothing more.

Elijah gripped my shaking hand and said, "Relax, I promise once you see him, the feeling will go away."

I glanced at the metal tables surrounding us, filled with families waiting for their loved ones just as we were, and then back at Elijah.

"This place is so cold." And I wasn't talking about the temperature.

"They don't make these places so that criminals can be comfortable, Lena," he said. I shook my head and frowned.

"Yea, but daddy didn't…" I let what was already known between the two of us hang in the air.

"You should've let Noah come back." I shook my head again.

"I needed to do this part without him," I repeated for the fifth time. "Knowing that he's just beyond the walls is enough for me." He opened his mouth to speak, but a loud, buzzing noise filled the room. A long line of inmates entered, shackled at the feet and hands. Tears immediately filled my eyes. Did they have to bring them in like that? There were children in here. Babies!

Elijah gripped my hand tighter, and I blinked back the tears. I hadn't even spotted him, and I was already emotional.

Jesus, please give me strength.

I let my eyes move from inmate to inmate until…

"Oh my God," I whispered, covering my mouth. Elijah chuckled and stood from his seat. I tried to follow suit, but my legs wouldn't allow me. My father looked the same as he did all those years ago when the police were hauling him out of our house on the west side of Detroit and pushing him into a cruiser. He was just an older version of that man. A salt and pepper beard littered his smooth, pecan colored face. His hair was cut down and looking fresh. Like he'd just hopped out of the barber's chair before walking in here. I knew they were creative in jail, but seeing it up close was something different. I watched in awe as he and Elijah embraced like there hadn't been any tension between them lately. When he looked over Elijah's shoulder at me, time stood still. And I was no good. With watery eyes clouding my vision, I smiled and waved.

Elijah walked toward me after breaking their embrace and pulled me from my seat.

"I promise it's OK," he whispered, pushing me toward my father. I inched forward, watching him intently, and then when I was closer, I jumped in his arms. When he wrapped those broad arms around me, I cried. Hard.

I tried to quickly gather myself because I knew they were strict about too much contact during visitation, and I didn't want to cause any problems for him.

"Daddy," I whispered, looking up into the eyes that matched mine.

"Hey, baby girl." His voice was deeper than I remembered. "Let's sit." I looked him over again and then nodded. I took my place next to Elijah, and he sat across from us. A few minutes went by with us, just staring at each other in silence. The noise surrounding us didn't even feel real. None of this did.

"You've grown up so much," he finally said. He looked over at Elijah. "The boys must—"

"I don't date boys," I quipped. He chuckled and nodded.

"My bad."

"I never had to worry about her," Elijah said. "She's tough." I smiled at my brother and then shifted my gaze back to my father. I still couldn't believe he was sitting in front of me looking well taken care of. It's like he hasn't been locked away all this time.

"I don't get it," I said. "I mean, this place definitely had me shook for a minute, but after seeing you, I don't understand what you were protecting me from." I placed my linked fingers onto the cold table and stared at him. "You look well, and I know that the conditions here are probably horrible, but *you* look fine."

The initial shock had worn off, and now I wanted answers. Needed them!

He rubbed a hand down his face, the same way Elijah does when he doesn't want to talk about something but is going to anyway. The gesture almost made me laugh.

"It never had anything to do with how I looked or even the conditions of this place if I'm laying it all out there." He sighed. "You were young when I came here. Thirteen and still impressionable. In the beginning, I wanted to shield you from this place simply because no child should have to see their parent like this." He looked around then paused on something. I followed his gaze and immediately knew what he meant. A guy was sitting to the left of us, holding what looked to be a newborn baby.

"I just—"

"That's Markell," he said, bringing his eyes back to me. "He was brought in here four months ago while his wife was seven months pregnant with their child. She died during childbirth, and they wouldn't let him attend the funeral."

My mouth parted in shock. I couldn't even fathom what that man was going through, but that poor baby was now parentless. I looked at the young woman sitting at the table with them.

"His oldest daughter is now a nineteen-year-old mother because no one else in his or his deceased wife's family wanted to take the baby in. She gave up going to college to take care of her."

Sheesh.

"I've watched him bury himself in regret for what he's caused. Of course, his daughter loves him, so she doesn't feel the same, but later on, down the line, she'll feel it. And when it hits her, she'll hate him for a while. She may even resent taking care of her baby sister. And to him, when that time comes, it'll again be all his fault."

"I would have never—" He cut me off with the shake of his head.

"You can't say that because that time never came," he said. "Had I let you come here when you were so young and still figuring life out, who knows what thoughts you may have had about me once you left."

"But you didn't even do it," I argued. He sliced a hand through the air.

"Doesn't matter because you didn't know that then. Until a few years ago, I was just your father, who was a murderer." I shook my head.

"You were never just that to me." Elijah grabbed my hand but kept quiet. "Not even before I knew."

"Because I protected you from feeling any other way."

"You wanted to preserve what she'd known you to be and not what this place turned you in to," Elijah said. "I get it."

"I wanted to protect you both, but I had a jilted way of doing it." He chuckled. "Double standards and shit."

"I'm trying to understand," I said. "I really am."

"It's alright if you don't."

"But—"

"I did what I felt was right at the time, and when you became of age, then it was more about me and less about the two of you." He crossed his arms. "Your brother wouldn't get the hint, so I told him the truth, and he still came around. I didn't have it in me to take him off the visitation list, but with you, I could still control that. I wanted to separate our worlds. You two were falling into your careers, growing and experiencing life. I wanted you to do it without thinking of me."

"Pop, you're talking in circles."

"I was at a tug-a-war with myself," he continued. "Depression hit me hard." He looked at me. "You were taking care of your mother, and that should have been my job. You should have been living your life." He glanced at Elijah. "You were fighting hard to keep a relationship between us, and I felt like I didn't deserve that."

"You felt unworthy of us," I whispered.

"Unworthy of you guys and life." My eyes widened.

"W-what?"

"I contemplated taking my own life on many nights. I even tried once."

"Pop—"

"No, you need to hear this," he said, cutting Elijah off. "I was sentenced fifteen to life with the possibility of parole eight years in." Elijah set up straighter. We'd known that, but he was denied parole. "I caused hell in this place right up until that point so that they'd deny me." He leaned in closer and whispered. "I needed to protect your mother."

"Even if you had been on your best behavior, they would have denied you anyway," Elijah said, frowning. "The system isn't built to give black men second chances."

"I did what I needed to either way, but afterward, I felt guilty for leaving the burdens of a husband on the two of you." It was all making sense now. "That's when the depression hit, and I couldn't let you guys see me like that."

"You let me come see you," Elijah pointed out.

"Like I said, I didn't have the guts to remove you from the list."

"So, you purposely did things that would make me not want to come." He nodded.

"Until I realized that wasn't the way." He tapped the table, and I smiled at the movement. I do the same when I'm deep in thought. He was so much like us. Or rather we were so much like him. "It wasn't until my baby girl started ignoring my calls that it hit me hard. I couldn't do it anymore."

"And here we are," I murmured. I glanced at Elijah to get a read on him and then focused my attention back on our father. "Just so you know, we still don't resent you."

"Even after everything, I'd just told you?" He looked back and forth between Elijah and me.

"Even then," Elijah said, standing. He held his hand out to our dad, who took it and stood along with him. This time when tears clouded my vision, I let them fall.

They hugged, and it felt like everything had fallen into place at that moment. Seconds later, Elijah was pulling me from my seat and into their embrace.

"That's enough," a guard yelled. We broke apart, and I stuck my tongue out at the guard, gaining laughter from my dad.

"Still feisty," he said.

"And never changing," I quipped, smiling. "Can we spend the rest of this visit catching up?" He nodded and smiled.

"I'd like that." We retook our seats, and he added, "You can tell me about the guy you have waiting for you out there."

"How did you—"

"I have eyes everywhere here." I rolled mine, and Elijah laughed. I jumped right into explaining who Noah was, and then Elijah brought him up to speed on his own life. This was what I wanted. But also it was what I needed.

I had said it before, and I'll say it again. We simply just needed our father, even if it was scheduled visits.

"Your mother is smiling down at this right now," he said, looking between the two of us with nothing but love shining through his gaze.

"Yea, I think so too," I said, agreeing.

An hour later, visitation was over, and we were being led toward the entrance. Once we were on the other side of the doors, my eyes searched for Noah. I found him just as he spotted me and began to make his way over. He gathered me into his arms and kissed my forehead. His eyes danced across my face, looking for any hint of sadness, but he wouldn't find any.

Furrowing his eyebrows, he asked, "You good?"

I nodded.

"Yea, baby," I answered. "I'm good." He kissed me again and nodded. "Let's go home."

"Let's do that." We walked hand in hand out of the building with Elijah following behind us. "You never cease to amaze me." I glanced his way with curious eyes. He shrugged. "I learn just how strong you are every day."

I smiled and looked away from him.

"There it is," he chimed.

"What?" He paused halfway to the car and gripped my shoulders.

"Sparkles, baby." My smile widened. *They were back.*

"Uno out!" Lilac yelled, jumping up from her place on the floor. "I told y'all you can't see me in this game."

"You do realize that you lost to Elena three times, and you only won this hand because she decided to sit this one out, right?"

"What's your point?" she asked Elijah as if he hadn't made it already. "I said y'all as in the people who are playing, not Elena." I laughed and shook my head. Lilac wasn't one who liked to lose, and if she did, she'd just pretend that it didn't happen. Elijah was slowly learning what the rest of us already knew. He threw his hands up with a smirk on his face.

"Whatever helps you sleep better at night," he mumbled.

"Let's just take shots and all be happy again," Blossom chimed in while passing out shot glasses to everyone.

"I'm good," I said, pushing her hand away. I glanced down at Elena, who had her head in my lap. "Are you drinking, baby?"

"No, I'm done for the night."

"You guys suck," Blossom said. "How can we have a successful game night without taking shots?"

"Samir and I are fasting so no liquor for us," Brynlee spoke from her spot on the other end of the couch. We were at my parent's beach house in New Jersey. The Game night was Elena's idea, and Nova suggested that we used this space because it was big enough to fit everyone comfortably. Her house would have been enough space too, but the beach house is an equal distance from New York and Philly.

I massaged Elena's scalp while taking in the room. It's been a week since the visit with her father, and she's been in a much better headspace. There was a day where she woke up crying, but I didn't expect anything less from her. I was a firm believer in time healing all wounds, and in this instance, a lot of time would be needed.

"OK, what game are we playing next?" Nova asked. Magnolia picked up a new Monopoly game that encourages you to cheat and held it up.

"I want to try this," she said. Everyone began to argue about what they wanted while Elena and I stayed silent. I leaned forward and pressed my lips to her exposed ear.

"I'm tired," I murmured. "What about you?" She nodded and lifted herself from the couch. I followed her lead, reaching for her hand once I was up. "Aye, we are headed to bed."

"What!" Juniper yelled, with a red cup gripped tight in her hand. "It's only…" she looked at her watch. "Two in the morning. It's—"

"Late," I said. "We'll catch y'all later for breakfast." I pulled Elena down the hall, not waiting for anyone else to protest. The beach house had three levels, six bedrooms, and the same amount of bathrooms to match. We were taking one of the rooms on the first floor.

"I'll never get over how beautiful this place is," Elena murmured after we locked ourselves in the room. "This is what it's like to have endless amounts of money." I glanced her way after pulling off my shirt and basketball shorts.

"It can end," I said, walking up behind her. She was standing near the terrace doors, peeking out. "Did you have fun today?" She turned to face me as I stepped closer. Her back hit the doors, and I swooped in, wrapping one of my arms around her body.

"Yes." When she looked up at me, the sparkle that'd been missing from her gaze was shining through brightly.

"I'll never get over how beautiful you are," I whispered. She was more than just her beauty, but that initial shock of how beautiful she was will never go away. That day had changed everything for me. I didn't feel it in that moment, but it happened. I was more sure of that now then I had been at that time.

"Noah," Brynlee called out, walking toward me. I heard her voice, but my eyes were trained on the brown-skinned beauty in red walking with her. I'd been watching her all night. I knew she was my sister's boyfriend's younger sister, but only knowing that about her wasn't enough. "Have you met, Elena?"

I held my hand out just as I had before and said, "We were introduced, but I feel like it wasn't properly." Brynlee laughed, and I knew it was accompanied with an eye roll.

"Is that so?" Elena asked in a soft tone.

"I think it is." She eventually took my hand and shook it.

"How do you suppose we change that?"

"I'm not sure yet, but when I find out, you'll be the first to know." She smiled and then slipped her hand from mine. Elena nervously looked around while I openly checked her out. "Has anyone ever told you that red is your color?"

That question may have sealed the deal for us. Her lips had quirked up and then spread into the broadest smile I'd ever seen on a woman before. She was radiating nothing but beauty.

"What are you thinking about?" Elena asked, bringing my attention back to her. She rubbed her fingers gently across my face, and I would be lying if I didn't say that I melted into the touch. This woman did things to me that no one had ever been able to achieve. In my instance, that one person who didn't need to be named anymore hadn't been to achieve. She made me feel like this love we shared could last more than fourteen years. That we were destined to love each other for a lifetime and then some.

"Just about how much I love you," I said. She smiled but lifted an eyebrow. "And about the first time we met."

"The first time our worlds shifted without our knowledge." I laughed and pulled her to the bed. I cut the lights out along the way, letting nothing but the moonlight from the terrace door seep into the room.

"Tell me something," she said, climbing underneath the blanket and sliding closer to me. She made herself comfortable in my arms and then tilted her head upward to give me her attention.

"Like?"

"Anything…" she paused and shook her head. "No, something you've never told me before."

I thought about what she was asking me for a minute, and only one thing came to mind.

"I used to think that love was a once in a lifetime type of thing. When my parents met, they were young. They fell in love, and that love is still there between them. There was even a time that they'd split, but eventually, they found their way back to each other. I thought that's what love was."

"And then?" I looked down at Elena and saw my future within those bright eyes of hers.

"And then the once in a lifetime love that I thought I'd found left me."

"But you thought she'd come back," she said.

"I did."

"And she did," she added, smiling. I couldn't help but toss her a smile back because I knew we were thinking the same thing. "I get where you're going."

"Yea?"

"Mmhm."

"So, you understand that you changed my view of love."

"Yes, I do." I didn't respond. There was no need to. We both understood what this was between us. I understood that eventually, this woman who had become my friend first would be my wife one day and the mother of my children. The thought of that made me want to stand in the middle of Time Square or at the top of the Empire State Building and shout to everyone that I'd found her. That I found my once in a lifetime love.

Yea, I still believed in it. Elena just made me realize that I'd chosen wrong the first time. She had been it all along.

"Noah?"

"Yes, baby?"

"Since we are speaking of love, I have something to tell you." She slipped away from me, and I turned my body sideways to face her. I laid my hand between us, and she took it. "I love you so much, Noah White."

"Is that what you had to tell me?" She smiled and chuckled. "I'll take that as a yes."

"Were you looking for more?"

"No, that was just enough," I replied, leaning in to kiss her face. "I love you just as much, Elena Brooks."

"Elena, your phone!" Noah yelled, walking into the kitchen. "Pretty sure it's your dad." I took the ringing iPhone from him and answered. While the automated system ran through its usual spiel, I stood on my tiptoes and poked my lips out for a kiss. Multiple groans filled the air, and I flipped everyone off.

"You love birds around here are sickening," Lilac said, gagging.

"Like seriously," Blossom cosigned, rolling her eyes. They had no idea what they were missing out on.

"Hey, dad," I chirped, once his voice boomed through the phone and into my ear. Everyone knew he was in jail, so I didn't feel the need to hide our conversation. Elijah walked over and leaned against the counter.

"Wassup, pop," he spoke, leaning his mouth toward the phone.

"Oh, good, y'all both are together," he said. "I have something to tell you."

Elijah couldn't hear what he was saying since the phone wasn't on, so I repeated what he'd said to him. We exchanged looks and then walked out of the kitchen with Nova and Noah following closely behind.

"Is it bad news?" I asked, placing it on speaker. We'd migrated into the office on the first floor. "Because I don't think I can take any more bad news this year." Noah's arms wrapped around my body from behind, and I leaned into him for support.

"Not quite bad," he said. "It's actually pretty great."

"OK," I said slowly. "Lay it on us."

"I'm being released this summer."

His words hit me like a freight train going a thousand miles per hour. I dropped my phone on the desk and covered my mouth.

"How did—when did…" Even Elijah was at a loss for words.

"It's a long story, and I'll explain in person because this timed call won't be enough," he said. "I just wanted you to know that your old man is coming home and…"

Nothing he had said after that registered. By the time I was able to focus on what was happening around me, the call had ended.

Holy fuck.

"This is really happening," I murmured, looking over at Elijah, who also looked just as shocked and confused as me. "He's coming home."

"Yea, sis," Elijah said. "He's coming home." I never expected that to be his news, but damn was it the best news I'd received lately. Noah's arms tightened around me, and I melted.

His lips were pressed to my ear as he said, "Life doesn't seem so bad after all, does it?" I turned to face him and pressed my chin into his chest.

"It was never bad," I said, shaking my head. "Not with you in it."

"Breakfast is done!" Magnolia yelled. "Better get in here before there's nothing left!"

Laughing, I looked around the office and took note that Elijah and Nova had already left.

"I guess we better get in there before Juniper eats all of the bacon," I said.

"Yea, we better." As we walked up the hall toward the kitchen hand in hand, I couldn't help but feel that everything would be alright. I missed my mother so much, but she hadn't died in vain. She made room on this earth for something great to happen. I could have never imagined things being this way, and I would forever be grateful.

"I love you," Noah said, squeezing my hand.

I glanced his way and replied, "I love you more."

And man did I mean that with all of my heart.

The End

Author Notes

You've made it to the end of Noah + Elena's story, and I truly hope you enjoyed it. Next up for me are the lovely flower sisters, which means we are headed to Philly for a little while. In the meantime, if you haven't already noticed, all of my old work had been removed from Amazon due to unforeseen circumstances. Since the removal, I have been able to acquire the publishing rights to those novels. I have slowly but surely been re-releasing said books, and your support has been much appreciated. Thank you.

Here are a few ways to stay connected with me:
Website: www.asiamonique.com
Like me on Facebook: http://bit.ly/AuthorAsiaMonique
Subscribe to my mailing list: http://eepurl.com/go_IYb
Join my readers group on Facebook:
http://bit.ly/ForTheLoveOfAsiaMonique
Follow me on Twitter & Instagram: www.
twitter.com/__ayemonique

Also By Asia Monique

About the Author

Asia Monique is a full-time student and romance author from Detroit, Michigan. Asia caters to creating love stories that shine a positive light on successful black men, and black love as a whole. She is currently obtaining a bachelor's degree in Creative Writing for Entertainment and plans to use that degree to break into the television industry. Asia is a lover of life, love, sports, music, and more.

CPSIA information can be obtained
at www.ICGtesting.com
Printed in the USA
LVHW081754061120
670969LV00012B/1561

9 781661 328269